"When

Poppy was lost. The hope in his eyes did something terminal to her insides, and that slight lift to his mouth—the cautious little twist that made her heart thud and her palms itch to cradle that firm, stubborn jaw—wiped away all her resolve. "That was a short interview," she said instead.

James grinned, and her last vestige of self-preservation puddled at her feet. "You want to be interviewed? Fine. Tell me, Miss Taylor, what makes you think you're qualified to look after my sons?"

She smiled weakly, and sat down at the table before her legs gave way. What had she let herself in for?

Caroline Anderson has the mind of a butterfly. She's been a nurse, a secretary, a teacher, run her own soft-furnishing business, and has now settled on writing. She says, "I was looking for that elusive something. I finally realized it was variety, and now I have it in abundance. Every book brings new horizons and new friends, and in between books I have learned to be a juggler. My teacher husband, John, and I have umpteen pets, two horse-mad daughters—Sarah and Hannah—and several acres of Suffolk that nature tries to reclaim every time we turn our backs! When I'm not writing, walking the dogs or waging war on the garden, I'm often driving around Suffolk behind the wheel of an ancient seven-and-a-half-ton horse lorry. Variety is a two-edged sword!"

Just Another Miracle!

Caroline Anderson

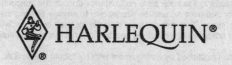

HARLEQUIN®

TORONTO • NEW YORK • LONDON
AMSTERDAM • PARIS • SYDNEY • HAMBURG
STOCKHOLM • ATHENS • TOKYO • MILAN • MADRID
PRAGUE • WARSAW • BUDAPEST • AUCKLAND

ISBN 0-373-17408-X

JUST ANOTHER MIRACLE!

First North American Publication 1999.

Copyright © 1998 by Caroline Anderson.

This edition published by arrangement with Harlequin Books S.A.

® and TM are trademarks of the publisher. Trademarks indicated with
® are registered in the United States Patent and Trademark Office, the
Canadian Trade Marks Office and in other countries.

Printed in U.S.A.

CHAPTER ONE

SHE should have known better.

If she hadn't been so busy ogling the elegant Georgian façade framed by that magnificent cedar tree, she might have paid more attention to the screaming of her instincts.

As it was, she was totally involved with rubbernecking at the glorious symmetry of the many-paned windows, admiring the architectural grace of the fanlight over the door and the echo it found in the wide sweep of gravel on which her mother's manky old runabout had now come to rest.

Oh, my, she thought. Oh, wow.

It was gorgeous. Not ostentatious, not pretentious, just beautiful enough to take her breath away, with the morning sun bathing the mellow cream bricks with gold and sparkling off the window-panes. She sucked in some much-needed air, then climbed out of the car, straightened her shoulders and marched up to the front door. It was slightly ajar, and she heard a clanging in the distance as she tugged the old bell-pull. In the silence that followed there was a muffled giggle.

'Hello? Is anybody there?' she called through the crack.

The giggle got louder, and was shushed vigorously.

She really *should* have known better. After all those years with Tom and David and Peter, she should have anticipated it—but she hadn't.

Pushing open the door cautiously, she stepped in—just as the bag of flour reached head height.

The giggles escalated to a shriek, followed by the thunder of running footsteps on the stairs.

Poppy didn't hesitate. Her wits firmly back in place, she kicked off her shoes and sprinted up the sweeping staircase after the villains.

A door slammed along to her right, and she whipped it open and caught them on the way into the wardrobe.

'Good morning, boys,' she said firmly, and hooked them out of their bolt-hole.

They were twins—that much was obvious. They had the skinny arms and legs of growing boys, and at rest their faces, under the wild mid-brown curls, would have been positively cherubic. However, for the first few seconds they were still caught in the high spirits of the prank, and devilment danced in their nut-brown eyes.

Poppy released them, folded her arms and waited.

The enormity of what they had done finally catching up with them, they at last stood motionless and stared at her flour-splattered form in awe.

'Well?' she prompted.

'Sorry,' they mumbled in unison.

'You will be. Who are you?'

'I'm George—'

'He's George.'

She turned to the one who wasn't George. 'And you are—?'

'William.'

'And are there any more of you?'

They shook their heads unhappily.

'Right, George and William, you have a little domestic task to perform, I believe?'

They gazed at her blankly.

'Cleaning up the mess?'

Their faces fell.

'Come on—downstairs, find a brush and sweep it up, then wash the floor. Good job it isn't carpet; you'd be brushing it for weeks.'

A hand firmly on each collar, she marched them downstairs to the marbled hall, helped them find the cleaning tools and then, retrieving her shoes, she disappeared into the cloakroom for some running repairs.

It was hopeless. She was dredged in flour, like icing sugar on a mince pie. Removing the worst from her shoulders with a few angry swipes, she uncoiled her now white hair, shook it over the basin and wound it back up again, securing it with a few hastily stabbed pins.

There was precious little trace of the dark honey-blonde she was used to seeing. Instead she looked like a refugee from a pantomime—Old Mother Hubbard or the Widow Twankee. And as for her clothes—!

There was no way she could create a good impression now, and no way she would even bother to try. Let him keep his job and his rotten, horrible little kids! TLC, indeed—

She yanked open the door and marched up the hall, heels clacking on the black and white marble slabs.

'Stick at it,' she told them grimly. 'Where's your father?'

They looked panic-stricken, and her anger faded slightly.

One of them—George, possibly?—pointed. 'In the library, over there—but you won't tell him, will you?'

'I hardly think that will be necessary, do you?' she said drily, and walking over to the heavy mahogany door he had indicated, she rapped sharply on it and went in.

He hadn't heard her knock. Either that or he'd ignored

it—no, he raised a hand in a 'hang on a tick' gesture and then dropped it again.

'That won't do—no, Mike. It has to be better than that.'

Poppy wondered idly what wouldn't do, and studied the progenitor of the horrors in the hall. At least, she assumed he was their progenitor—or was the word she was looking for 'perpetrator'? That usually applied to the person committing a crime. Yes, she thought, perpetrator fits.

He sat with his back to her in a large swivel chair, his feet propped on the edge of a huge mahogany desk, telephone in hand. It was obviously a business call, so Poppy let him get on with it. There would be plenty of time for the little she had to say.

She tried to imagine what he would look like from the front. Difficult with such a restricted view.

He was big, she could see that instantly, even from the small amount of him that was visible over the high leather back of the chair. And definitely the boys' father. The short brown curls that rampaged over his head gave that away.

How old? Thirty? Thirty-five? she speculated. Somewhere round there. Not older. His voice was deep, confident, assertive, the voice of a man who knew what he wanted and meant to have it. His hair was thick, and looked soft and glossy, with no visible signs of balding—yet. She'd probably change all that in a moment.

Eye colour? Blue, she decided, ice-blue to go with that commanding voice—that slightly exasperated, commanding voice. His nose would have been broken at some time—probably because he had tried to dominate some ungrateful peer at school who had failed to appreciate him. His lips would be full—no, perhaps not. Firm, though, with a decisive set. He didn't smile often, even though he had a sense of humour.

Poppy wondered how she could tell that from the dry conversation she was forced to eavesdrop. There was no humour in it, no humour at all.

But there had been in the advert, she reminded herself. One of her brothers had pointed it out to her in *The Lady* the night before.

'''ARE YOU OUT THERE, MARY POPPINS?''' Tom had read. '''We're good kids really, we just need a firm hand and a little bit of TLC.'''

'Oh, yeah?' David had snorted. 'That's given the advert the kiss of death!'

'I could do with a little tender loving care,' Peter put in.

'More like the firm hand,' his father commented drily from the depths of *Farmers' Weekly*.

'Hush, all of you. This looks interesting. Anyway, they couldn't be worse than you lot. "Own flat, car, excellent pay and conditions—and if you can cook better than Dad, we'll all be grateful!"' She put the paper down and looked round at her expectant family. 'I wonder where it is?'

'Who it is, more importantly,' her father said. 'Sounds like a widower or divorcee—'

'Whoopee! A little love interest for big sister!'

'You mean s—'

'Thomas! That'll do—and get your feet off the table!' Audrey Taylor reached across and swatted at her son's toes. The chair-legs hit the floor with a crash. 'What else does it say?'

Poppy made a little face. 'Nothing. There's a phone number with a Norwich code. That would be handy, just as a stop-gap until September.'

Her last nannying job had come to an end weeks ago when the family went abroad. She'd spent Christmas at home on the Taylors' Suffolk farm, but now it was time to find something else to do just until she started college after the summer—if she did decide to go.

She eyed the advert, her interest piqued, and wondered who had placed it. Whoever they were, they had a sense of humour, she thought. 'It won't hurt to ring,' she said with a dismissive little shrug, and, picking up the paper, she went out of the big rambling kitchen and into the farm office.

A large, sleek ginger cat was coiled comfortably on the chair, and she dumped him on the floor. Offended, he stalked off, tail high, the tip twitching reproachfully at her as she dialled the number in the advert.

There was no reply. At eight-thirty on a Friday evening, they were probably out somewhere. Conscious of a vague feeling of disappointment, she was about to hang up when there was a clatter from the other end and a voice shrieked, 'I've got it!'

She closed her eyes and switched sides with the phone, rubbing the insulted ear ruefully.

'Hello, could I speak to—'

'Dad's just coming, hang on. It's a woman.'

'Right—get into bed. Hello?'

The voice was deep and gravelly, sexy as all get out and harassed to death. Poppy's lips twitched.

'It's Mary Poppins,' she said. 'I believe you're having a little difficulty?'

There was a strangled sound from the other end that could just have been laughter. Then again, it could just as easily have been despair.

'You might say that,' he agreed. 'Look, I can't really talk now—when are you available to start?'

Poppy blinked. Just like that? 'Now,' she said
promptly.

'Fine—could you come for an interview tomorrow
morning? Say, nine o'clock?'

And so here she was, wondering how she had thought
he had a sense of humour. Probably his secretary had
drafted the advert. If so, she was way off the mark. A
little bit of TLC? Those kids in the hall needed more
than tender loving care. They needed boot camp—and
the man with his back to her probably needed a loboto-
my.

She took a few seconds out to admire the sheer
breadth of the charcoal-grey suit stretched taut over
those rather fascinating shoulders. After all, there was
nothing else to do but wait.

It was a good suit. It had that faint sheen of pure wool,
perhaps with a touch of silk, and it fitted him beautifully.
It seemed a little excessive for a Saturday morning at
home with twin boys of about eight, but that didn't stop
Poppy admiring it, and wondering how that fine, soft
fabric would feel under her fingers—

Dragging her eyes from his shoulders, she looked
round the room. You could tell a lot about a person from
their home ground. She, for instance, was a natural
hoarder and couldn't resist a good junk-sale. Scanning
the magnificent room, she doubted this man had been to
a junk-sale in his life.

The walls were lined with shelves, except for the
chimney breast which housed a beautiful and very simple marble fire surround with a heavy cast-iron black
grate that she guessed hardly ever saw a fire. There were
bits of paper screwed up and chucked at it, some in the
grate, others on the tiled hearth, and an old oil painting
of a bowl of overblown roses hung over the mantelpiece.

Beside it was a big, comfy sofa with a stack of papers at one end and a heap of crushed cushions in the corner—obviously a favourite perch. Otherwise the room was empty except for the desk and the books.

Stuffed to bursting, the enormous old mahogany shelves gleamed with the patina of age, but the books were modern, a vast collection of well-thumbed tomes on an eclectic range of topics. She pulled out one on Suffolk houses and flicked through it.

He was winding up now, so she waited until he hung up.

'Not now, boys,' he muttered, punching in fresh numbers on the phone. 'I'll be out soon.'

Boys? 'Ahem,' she said pointedly, and shut the book with a snap.

The chair spun round, and she met his eyes with commendable composure.

Hazel, she thought, not blue. Hazel. Lovely, rich nut-brown and olive-green shot through with gold, and rimmed by dark brown lashes that she would cheerfully have sold her soul for.

After a second or two in which those hazel eyes tracked disbelievingly over her ruined clothes, he looked back to her face, his expression stunned.

'Good Lord! What happened to you?'

'I've been making pastry,' she said sarcastically. 'I believe you were expecting me? I'm—'

'Mary Poppins. I know. I recognise the voice—you're late.'

She arched a slim brow. 'Actually I was early—perhaps unfortunately. Had I been late you might have intercepted the crisis.'

He set his pen down with great deliberation. 'So what happened,' he asked slowly. 'Or don't I want to know?'

'You need to ask?'

'You've met the clones.' He dragged a hand down his face. 'Look, I'm sorry—'

'So am I. I just wanted to let you know that they're clearing up the mess at the moment, and I'm going. Goodbye.'

She turned towards the door but he was there first, his large hand reaching over her head to hold it shut.

'Wait—please. I'm sorry you've got off to a shaky start—'

'Shaky?' Poppy almost laughed out loud. 'Look at me, for goodness' sake!' She let her breath out on a sigh and turned to face him—and swallowed. She was used to big men—God knows, her brothers all towered over her, but they had the lightness of youth. This man—good grief, he was huge! 'Mr...?'

'Carmichael—'

'Mr Carmichael, while you were sitting in here in your ivory tower, those children were running wild out there. They could have been in danger.'

A muscle worked in his jaw. 'I wasn't far away.'

'No, but you were oblivious. You can't afford to take your eyes off them for a moment—'

'How dare you walk in here, knowing nothing of the situation, and presume to tell me about my obligations?' he demanded savagely, his voice rising.

His firm, full mouth was set in an uncompromising line, and he was angry—livid, in fact.

She stood her ground.

'Don't shout at me because you've got a guilty conscience!' she retaliated hotly. 'I dare because when I innocently crossed your threshold I was flour-bombed by a booby-trap set by your sons, and you knew nothing

about it! Lord knows what other mischief they might get
up to unchecked—'

'Damn it, I don't need lessons in childcare from some
little slip of a thing not much more than a girl herself!'
he retorted angrily. 'I didn't advertise for a nanny because I could cope without one!'

Poppy tipped back her head and met his eyes, her own
flashing blue sparks. She took a steadying breath and
deliberately lowered her voice, regaining control of the
situation.

'Well, I wish you luck with your search, Mr
Carmichael,' she said, with all the dignity she could
muster. 'It'll be a very special person who can cope with
your family. Excuse me, please.'

She looked pointedly at his hand on the door, and after
a second he dropped it and yanked the door open.

Drawing herself up to her full five feet seven, she
nodded coolly and walked out into the hall.

The boys were standing in a muddle of mops and
brooms, their eyes like saucers.

'Sorry, Dad,' they mumbled unhappily.

'I'll deal with you two later—go to your room!' he
thundered.

They fled, pausing on the half-landing to poke out
their tongues.

It was a foolish move. With a muttered oath he started
towards the staircase, but Poppy had seen the fear behind
the defiant little gesture, and she caught his arm, blocking his way.

'Don't,' she urged. 'They're only attention-seeking.
Anger's the last thing they need. Wait until you've
cooled off and then go and talk to them.'

She sensed the internal struggle that lasted a few seconds, and then his shoulders sagged and his face registered defeat.

'I'm sorry. You're right, of course.' His breath left him in a rush. 'Forgive me—can we start again?'

His smile was tentative, almost rusty, and Poppy felt something inside her give way. 'I think that would be a good idea.' She smiled back.

Respect dawned in the warm hazel eyes. He thrust out his hand.

'James Carmichael.'

'Poppy Taylor.' His hand was hard and warm, engulfing hers in a firm grip. To her surprise the warmth spread up her arm and suffused her cheeks. She eased her hand away and tucked it out of mischief in her pocket.

'Are you going to save my life, Poppy Taylor?' he asked lightly, but there was a hint of desperation in his voice.

She almost laughed. Here he was, ten times their size, obviously a powerful and successful man, and reduced to chaos by the antics of two small boys!

'Is it really that bad?'

He snorted. 'At least! Why don't I tell you all about it over a coffee?'

'Thank you, that would be lovely.'

She followed him out to the big old-fashioned kitchen in the back part of the house, and closed her eyes.

It looked as if a culinary bomb had gone off.

'Sorry, my cleaning lady's been off sick for a week and it's got a little out of hand,' he explained lamely.

Poppy blinked. A little?

Why was it that a man who was so obviously highly capable should be so completely at sea when faced with domesticity? she wondered.

He pushed a pile of clothes off one of the chairs and held it out for her.

'Have a seat. I'll find the coffee.'

'Shall I wash up some of the mugs?' she suggested, and he agreed with such alacrity she almost laughed aloud.

He put the kettle on and then found a teatowel, coming to stand beside her and dry the mugs as she washed them.

There was something about the simple, homely task that broke down barriers, Poppy had always thought. This occasion was no exception.

'I'm really sorry about the boys,' he said after a moment, and there was no doubting the sincerity of his apology. 'You've been very reasonable.'

'I've got three younger brothers,' she told him by way of explanation.

'Ah,' he said. That was all, but they exchanged a wealth of understanding in the smiles that followed.

'So,' she said after a moment, 'how come you need a nanny?'

His smile faded. 'I'm a widower—my wife died five years ago when the boys were three. We had a housekeeper, and she had a niece who looked after the boys during the day until they went to school. After that I had an au pair, but that didn't work. Since then they've had a succession of nannies and helpers and God knows what during the holidays, and the last nanny...' He hesitated, his mouth tightening into a firm line. 'Let's just say she left rather suddenly in August.'

'Oh.'

'Oh, indeed. Right in the summer holidays. I managed to persuade my old prep-school headmaster to take the boys as boarders from September, but they didn't settle well. I sent them back at the start of this term, hoping it would go rather better, but the head rang me last week and asked me to take them away.'

'Were they unhappy?' she asked sympathetically.

'Not as unhappy as he was—they'd found some white paint and written something unrepeatable on the cedar shingles of the cricket pavilion.'

Poppy stifled a smile.

James picked up another mug and dried it thoughtfully. 'It wouldn't have been so bad,' he added, 'if they'd been able to spell the word.'

She laughed then, a little bubble of fun that refused to be suppressed, and he shot her a wry grin.

'It's funny now, but it wasn't,' he went on. 'My housekeeper, who was nearly sixty, had decided at Christmas that she was going to retire—with immediate effect. That meant I would have no one here except the rather forbidding Mrs Cripps, so I had to drive down to Kent, pick the boys up from school and bring them back and somehow get them into another school as quickly as possible, and keep the business running and sort out the domestic arrangements. Then Mrs Cripps decided it was all too much and she was going off sick...' He shrugged helplessly. 'You see why I need a nanny.'

Poppy shook her head. 'You don't need a nanny, Mr Carmichael,' she told him frankly. 'You need a miracle.'

'What—just another miracle? I'd order it but I seem to have lost the phone number.' He turned towards her and she was touched by the bleakness in his eyes that underlined the bitter sadness of his remark. 'I'm sorry they put you off. I had such hopes—still.'

He set the mug down and sighed, then reached for the instant coffee.

'I don't suppose you know a paragon of virtue who's fool enough to take us on?'

Poppy had done some idiot things in her time, but she had a feeling they would pale into insignificance any second.

'As a matter of fact, I do.'

He turned his head. 'You do?'

She smiled faintly.

He regarded her in silence for a second, then hope flickered like a pale flame in the back of those beautiful eyes. The corner of his mouth lifted slightly, and the years seemed to fall away. 'When can you start?'

Poppy was lost. The hope in his eyes did something terminal to her insides, and that slight lift to his mouth— the cautious little twist that made her heart thud and her palms itch to cradle that firm, stubborn jaw—it wiped away all her resolve. She opened her mouth to retract her words, but it betrayed her.

'That was a short interview,' she said instead.

He grinned, and her last vestige of self-preservation puddled at her feet. 'You want to be interviewed? Fine. Tell me, Miss Taylor, what makes you think you're qualified to look after my sons?'

She smiled weakly, dried her hands and sat down at the table before her legs gave way. What had she let herself in for?

He put a mug of coffee in front of her, hitched up a chair and turned it round, straddling the seat and folding his arms along the back. He had shed his suit jacket and turned back the cuffs on his undoubtedly pure silk shirt, and she found herself suddenly fascinated by the soft curls that dusted his powerful forearms and sprinkled the backs of his large hands with their slender, blunt-tipped fingers—

'Well?'

Poppy blinked.

'Your qualifications?'

'Oh—yes. Um—I've done a two-year nursery nurse training and worked for six years as a nanny—the last two and a half with the same family. The children ranged from eighteen months to nearly teens. On top of that, I've helped my mother with my three younger brothers, so I think I'm fairly familiar with the convoluted workings of a child's mind!'

He gave a wry snort. 'Thank God for that! One of us needs to be. OK, so you're qualified. Can you cook?'

She smiled slightly. 'Better than you, I imagine, if the advert was anything to go by! What do you have in mind in the way of domestic duties?'

He lifted one shoulder expressively. 'Not a lot. There's a cleaning lady—the aforementioned Mrs Cripps—five mornings a week to do the basics. It would only be a question of cooking for the family, and a lot of the time I'm out. The boys will be at school all day, so it's a doddle.'

She looked round at the chaotic kitchen. 'It is?'

He gave a helpless shrug. 'If you have that sort of mind. I don't.'

She met his eyes with a level look. 'I can see that,' she said drily. 'OK, when would you want me to start?'

'Don't you want to know about your salary or see the flat or whatever?'

She arched a brow. 'Are you intending to cheat me?'

He snorted. 'Me?' His mouth curved in a wry grin. 'No, Mary Poppins, I'm not intending to cheat you. I'm just only too grateful that you'll take us on. As for starting—whenever you like. I'll have to get a signature from you for the bank, so you can use the household account, but there's a cashpoint card with it so if you can manage with that for a few days it would help.'

'You're very trusting.'

Their eyes locked. 'I'm a big man, Miss Taylor. Anybody who'll stand toe to toe with me and remind me of my obligations has integrity enough for me.'

She flushed. 'I should never had said all that...'

'Forget it. You were absolutely right; I know that. I've done my damnedest, but it hasn't been enough. Perhaps you'll sort us all out.'

He stood up, tall and powerful and very close, and gestured towards a door. 'Let me show you the flat.'

They went up the back stairs to a small suite of rooms over the kitchen area. There was a good-sized sitting room with a window overlooking the garden, and a neat little bedroom beside it, both recently decorated with fresh, pretty florals and soothing pastel accents. The bathroom was small but spotlessly clean, and there was even a tiny kitchen.

Poppy's heart lifted. By the time she'd filled it with her possessions, the little flat would be just like home. She could picture herself curled up on the chair by the window, a cracking good romance in one hand and a steaming mug of cocoa in the other, the boys asleep, and maybe even on occasions James opposite her in the other chair, a game of chess under way on the low table between them.

She'd have to let him win, of course, but perhaps not always. The occasional victory would go a long way to make up for his first impression of her as a flour-dredger.

'It's lovely,' she told him. 'Just fine.' She turned, a smile ready on her lips, and faltered.

He must have been standing right behind her because he was scant inches away, his big body almost completely blocking the tiny hallway. She stepped back and stumbled, and his big hands came out and caught her shoulders, saving her from falling. Somehow her hands ended up on his chest, and the heat of his body through the fine silk shirt almost burned her palms.

'Steady,' he murmured, and that deep chocolate voice melted over her nerve-endings and jammed the air in her lungs.

Poppy took a deep breath. It was a mistake. He smelt warm and clean and masculine, untouched by any artificial fragrance, his scent wholly exclusive and absolutely intoxicating.

Her heart crashed against her ribs, and she felt the most absurd urge to lean against him until the strength returned to her disobedient legs. Their eyes met, and after an endless, heartstopping moment, in which Poppy wondered rather wildly if he would kiss her, he released her gently and moved away.

'I'm glad you like it,' he said, his voice carefully neutral. 'I don't know when you want to start—as you can see, we're ready whenever you are.'

Her stupid heart fell. So he wasn't going to kiss her after all. Damn. 'Fine,' she replied, her voice as light as she could manage. 'Shall I move in this afternoon?'

'That would be excellent. You can bring your own car if you like, but there's one here for your use on or off duty—unless you're going to tell me you can't drive anything bigger than a shopping trolley?'

Poppy's lips twitched. 'If it's smaller than a combine harvester, I'm sure I'll manage!'

He laughed then, and Poppy felt the tension ease a little. 'Somewhat smaller,' he agreed.

She followed him down the stairs and out into the hall. The evidence of the booby-trap was still strewn around the floor, which was now coated with generous dollops of flour and water paste. It looked like the aftermath of a nursery school *papier mâché* session, and Poppy had no illusions about how difficult it would be to remove all traces of the flour from the black marble squares.

'Don't be too hard on them,' she said gently. 'I'd like to get off to a good start with your boys, and if they think I've got them into awful trouble, it'll just make it all the harder.'

He moved a mop out of the way with his foot and opened the front door for her. 'I promise not to break any bones,' he said with the merest trace of a smile in his eyes.

She smiled back. 'You do that. I'll see you this afternoon.'

'I'll look forward to it.'

He shook her hand, his warm and firm, the fingers strong but gentle. She turned away and ran down the steps to the car, conscious of a tremble in her fingers as she fumbled the key into the ignition, still vitally aware of the imprint of his palm on hers.

Was she mad? She could feel her pulse race, the surge of adrenaline that came with anticipation—but of what? As she drove away, she wondered how much of that anticipation was to do with the boys and how much to do with the glimpse of vulnerability she had seen in their father's astonishingly beautiful eyes...

CHAPTER TWO

TOM was in the office, fair hair rumpled, a glower fixed firmly on his usually cheerful face. He looked up at Poppy as she went in, and his jaw sagged.

'What the bloody hell happened to you?' he asked in astonishment.

'I was interviewed,' she said sweetly.

'What for—one of these Japanese game shows?'

Poppy laughed. 'Something like that.'

'And did you pass?'

Her smile faded. 'Yes, I passed. I'm not so sure about them. It'll certainly be a challenge.'

'So you're taking it?'

She nodded. 'Yes—I start this afternoon. Can you run me over there so I don't have to worry about returning the car? There's one I can use, apparently.'

Tom brightened visibly at the thought of escaping from the farm accounts for a while. 'My pleasure.'

Poppy winked at him. 'I won't keep you long, brother dear.'

'Shame—what's for lunch?'

'Don't know,' she called over her shoulder. 'Ask Mum—I'm packing!'

An hour later her most essential possessions were packed and in Tom's car. The rest would keep till she had some time off.

Humming cheerfully, she went into the big kitchen.

'You sound happy,' her mother said with a smile. 'Tom said you got the job.'

'Mmm. I just hope I'm man enough for it.'

'Poppy, didn't anyone ever tell you the facts of life?' Peter quipped, lifting his nose from a lurid thriller.

'Ha-ha. Have you done your homework yet?' she retaliated.

He groaned. 'When did you say you're leaving?'

'After lunch. Smells good, what are we having?'

'Vegetable soup,' her mother said, dumping a big tureen in the centre of the table and dishing up brimming bowls of thick, steaming broth. 'So, tell us all about it—what's his name?'

'James Carmichael. He's a widower, twin boys of eight, lovely house set in several acres of grounds—must have pots of money.'

David raised his head from his soup and frowned. 'Not the computer boffin?'

'Could be, I suppose—I didn't ask him what he did.'

'Big bloke, brown curly hair, cut short—early thirties?'

Poppy shrugged. 'Could be—why, what do you know about him?'

David quirked an eyebrow. 'You haven't heard of him? Where have you been living? Not that he has a very high profile; he's a very private man by all accounts.'

'Obviously,' Poppy said drily. 'So private he's unheard-of.'

David snorted. 'Hardly. He just doesn't socialise much. Commercially he's red-hot. Dynamite. He made his money in computer software for industry. He's revolutionised office management—simple, easy to operate programs, very user-friendly. Now he's moved into the multimedia market and he's cleaning up big-time.' He shrugged expressively. 'The guy's a legend.'

Poppy's lips twitched. 'Well, he might have revolutionised office management, but he can't manage two small boys to save his life!'

'No?' her mother asked curiously. 'What makes you say that?'

She laughingly explained about the flour-bomb and her ensuing interview with the embarrassed Mr Carmichael, while her family rolled around and clutched their sides.

'Do you remember when we did that?' David wheezed.

Tom hooted. 'Yeah—with a bucket of water, and the bucket knocked her out and she had to go to Casualty!'

'I hadn't forgotten,' Poppy said drily. 'I had six stitches in my head and I was concussed for a week!'

'Let's hope he's well insured,' Peter put in cheerfully. 'You could make a packet, Pops.'

'Thank you, little brother. Your concern is touching, but my instinct for self-preservation is back in full force.'

'If they're anything like your brothers, you'll need it,' her father said mildly.

They bantered and bickered their way through lunch, and then it was finished and Poppy was hugging them all goodbye and being wished luck and told to break a leg and keep in touch and so on.

As they pulled up outside the house, Tom looked around and gave a low whistle.

'Nice, isn't it?' Poppy said with a grin.

'Nice? Where do you find your vocabulary?'

Tom shouldered open the door and pulled Poppy's bags out of the back of the car, then followed her to the front door.

The bell jangled, and then they heard a door slam and

the thunder of footsteps. Almost instantly the door was flung back on its hinges and two mischievous little faces grinned up at them.

'Still alive?' Poppy teased.

'Just barely.' Carmichael appeared behind them and winked at her, then turned to her companion. 'You must be one of the brothers.'

Poppy introduced them and watched as they shook hands, each weighing the other one up. How long they would have stood there like stags at bay Poppy didn't like to imagine, but she cut the confrontation short by handing a small bag to each of the boys and suggesting they should show them the way to the flat.

Carmichael took a bag from Tom and followed the boys up the sweeping staircase, past the massive leaded window that looked out over the garden.

'Nice place you've got here,' Tom said conversationally, eyeing the surroundings with obvious mistrust.

'We like it. Here we are—right, boys, put the bags down and let's leave Miss Taylor in peace to unpack for a few minutes.'

They left her and Tom alone, and Poppy rolled her eyes. '"Nice place you've got here,"' she mimicked. 'Really, Tom, where do you get your vocabulary?'

He ignored her. 'Is there anybody else here?'

'I don't think so—a cleaning lady every morning, but otherwise I think it's just us.'

'Cosy.'

'Tom, spit it out—'

'OK. I didn't like the way he winked at you.'

Poppy laughed.

'Well, I didn't. It was suggestive.'

'You're being absurd! Anybody would think he leered!'

'The man has money. He doesn't have to leer.'

'I'm not influenced by his money. Money isn't important to me.'

'You could get used to what it provides.' Tom picked up a cushion and inspected it minutely. 'Poppy, he's very...'

'Very...?'

'Well —masculine...you know. Don't tell me you hadn't noticed.'

A faint flush touched her cheeks. 'So he's masculine—so what? That doesn't mean he's about to take advantage of our relationship and seduce me!' She took the cushion away from her brother and hugged him. 'Trust my judgement—the man is so desperate for a nanny he isn't about to put a foot wrong.'

Tom snorted with disbelief.

'Trust me,' she said again with a comforting smile.

'Oh, I trust *you*, Poppy.' He hugged her tight, then released her a little awkwardly. Poor Tom. He'd never known what to do with her since she'd sprouted a chest and shot up nine inches in two years. Even after all this time he still hadn't got the hang of hugging her without blushing.

He brushed her cheek with his knuckles. 'You call me if he gives you any grief, OK?'

'He won't—'

'Promise.'

She sighed. 'I promise. Now go away and stop bristling, and let me get on with my life. I'm twenty-five, for heaven's sake!'

She took him back downstairs and stood on the drive, watching him out of sight. Then with a sigh and a fond shake of her head, she turned back to the front door.

'He's very protective.'

Poppy looked up and smiled apologetically. 'I'm
sorry—I didn't realise it showed that badly.'

Carmichael's mouth tilted at one side. 'That's OK—
I'd be the same if you were my sister.'

He held the front door for her with what she was
beginning to realise was habitual and absolutely natural
courtesy. As she passed him in the doorway, he took her
arm and halted her.

'You're quite safe, Poppy—in spite of what happened
upstairs this morning. I want you to know that.'

Her heart thumped. So she hadn't imagined it after
all! She made herself meet his eyes, then looked quickly
away.

'Thank you. I wouldn't be here if I didn't think I was.'

'I just wanted you to know.'

He released her and turned away to the library.

'Make yourself at home,' he threw over his shoulder.
'I'll see you when you're all sorted out.'

She went back upstairs to her little flat and unpacked
her 'essentials'—photos of family and friends, an old
teddy, her jeans and sweatshirts and jogging pants, one
skirt, a few blouses and her trainers, and some basics for
the kitchen: tea, coffee, milk powder. She stacked her
bottles and potions in the bathroom on the little corner
shelf, and then that was it.

Taking her courage in both hands, she decided to go
and find out what her charges were up to. That was, after
all, why she was here...

Poppy found the children in the garden, mud up to their
ears, constructing a dam over a little stream.

'Dad wants you,' one of them said. She looked hard
at him.

'William?'

He grinned. 'That's right—how did you guess?'

'I didn't—you're quite different in a similar sort of way.'

'Dad gets us mixed up,' George told her. 'Sometimes we tease him.'

She allowed a small smile to emerge. 'I'll just bet you do. Do you know where he is?'

'Kitchen,' William told her. 'He's making tea. He's not very good at it; you're better off doing it yourself.'

'I'm sure it will be fine,' she said, quelling the mutiny before it got under way. 'I'll go and see.'

'Miss Taylor?'

She turned back. 'Yes?'

'Thanks for not letting us put you off—Dad would've killed us if you hadn't asked him not to—he said so.'

She chuckled. 'I'm sure he wouldn't, really—and call me Poppy. Miss Taylor makes me feel dreadfully old.'

She made her way back to the kitchen and let herself in. 'I gather you're looking for me,' she told her new employer.

He was standing in his socks, polishing a pair of shoes, and he looked suddenly curiously approachable. He glanced up at her briefly. 'Sort of. I thought you might want me to show you the ropes, but as what I know about running this house could be written on the head of a pin you'll probably do better finding it all out for yourself. I've just made some tea,' he added.

'Yes—the boys told me.'

He looked up at her again and locked her with the laserbeam of his gorgeous eyes. Humour glimmered in their gold-green depths. 'Did they also tell you I make lousy tea?'

She was too slow to stop the smile.

He laughed wryly. 'Here—feel free to chuck it down the sink.'

She let the smile grow, fascinated by the crows' feet round his eyes and the rich timbre of his laugh. 'I'm sure it will be fine. Nobody can ruin tea,' she said optimistically.

She poured herself a cup and sat down at the table, watching him. He worked efficiently, his movements brisk and economical. He was standing with his back to her and she let her eyes track over the breadth of his shoulders, following the tapering line of his body down to the neat waist and slim hips encased in well-cut charcoal-grey trousers. The suit, still? Probably.

Even so, despite the jet-set Alpha-personality uniform, he didn't look like a typical desk-bound executive, she thought absently. There wasn't an ounce of fat on him anywhere, and out of nowhere she remembered the feel of his chest, hard and hot beneath her palms, and the steady beat of his heart. Was that really only this morning? She felt her cheeks heat with the memory.

Enough, she chided herself. The last thing she needed was input from her hormones!

Distracted, she sipped the tea and pulled a face. The boys were right—it was awful! She pushed it away.

'Are you the computer boffin?' she asked suddenly.

A brow quirked. 'Boffin? I design software, that's all. I wouldn't say I was a boffin.'

'My middle brother said you were a legend.'

She was fascinated by the slow run of colour that crawled up his neck.

'Slight exaggeration,' he said drily. 'Let's just say I've made some lucky career moves.'

She changed tack. 'About my flat—'

He turned his head, his brow creased. 'Is there a problem?'

'Oh, no—no, not at all. I just wondered if I would eat with you all, or up there, and where I can go in the house—that sort of thing. I don't want to be underfoot.'

'Why not?' he countered. 'The boys are, constantly. If you're to look after them and do your job properly, you'll have to have the run of the house.'

He dropped his shoes to the floor and pushed his feet into them, then crouched to tie them. Poppy watched the silk shirt strain over the muscles of his back and thought she would have to burn it in the interests of her sanity, then decided it wouldn't help. He'd look good in sackcloth and ashes.

'I want us to have as much family life as possible,' he was saying. 'I know it isn't easy with me out so much, and just at the moment I'm away for days at a time, but they need continuity. That's your job. How you do it is up to you.'

He took a mouthful of tea, grimaced at the cup and tossed the contents into the sink.

Poppy stifled a smile. 'I expect it was cold—would you like me to make you some fresh?'

'I thought you'd never ask,' he confessed with a chuckle. 'I'll be in the library—come and join me. We can sort out the bits and pieces.'

The 'bits and pieces' turned out to be handing over the keys of the 'little' Mercedes, giving her a map of Norwich so she could find the boys' school, amongst other things, getting her to fill in her bank details for his personnel department so that she would get paid on time, and agreeing a salary.

Her agreement on the latter was tacit. She was too

stunned to argue. He eyed her open mouth and laughed without humour.

'You'll earn it—if you stay that long.'

By the time she had got the boys to bed that night, cleared up the kitchen and gone to bed herself, she began to think he was right.

They had obviously decided that they had crawled enough, and were reverting to type. That was fine. Poppy could deal with small boys and healthy high-jinks. She was just a little out of practice.

'Give me a week,' she said to herself as she snuggled down in the warm bedroom under the down-filled duvet. 'I'll get them in line.'

Poppy always had been optimistic. That first week showed her how wide of the mark her optimism could be.

Carmichael got the week off to a flying start by announcing on Sunday morning that, as she was obviously very capable, he would go to New York as planned on Monday morning, arriving back on Friday evening.

By Friday night, she was tearing her hair out. At nine the phone rang. It was her boss, back at Norwich airport after a delay in Amsterdam, and could she pick him up as the taxis were all busy?

'The boys are in bed asleep; you'll have to wait for one,' she told him shortly, and hung up.

He arrived half an hour later, by which time she was regretting her impulsive behaviour, and found her in the kitchen.

'Something wrong?' he asked quietly.

She shrugged. 'The boys had a fairly rough week at school. I'm sorry I snarled at you. I've been worried about them.'

'How, rough?'

'You know, attention-seeking little numbers like wetting all the chalk and putting red in the white powder paint and scribbling on the reading books—have you eaten?'

He shrugged off his jacket and dropped into a chair. 'Yes, I've eaten. I could use a drink.'

'Tea or coffee?'

'Scotch—malt, half a tumbler, as it comes.'

'Is that wise?'

He swore softly under his breath. 'Poppy, I don't need nannying. No, I don't suppose it is wise, but I've had a hell of a week, a lousy flight and I've had it up to here.'

She found the malt whisky in the sitting room and poured him a compromise. He eyed it, snorted quietly and raised the glass.

'Cheers, Poppy. Happy days.'

Poppy's soft heart went out to him. He looked exhausted, at the end of his tether, and he really didn't need her lecturing him on the shortcomings of his offspring.

'Somebody called Helen rang—she said don't let you forget tomorrow night.'

'What? Oh, damn. Dinner. Oh, well, I'll see her in the office tomorrow, no doubt.'

'Office?'

'Yes—I'll have to go in all day and catch up. Maybe even Sunday as well.'

Poppy was horrified. 'Mr Carmichael, the boys are dying to see you. They've missed you.'

He loosened his tie, undid the collar of his shirt and sighed heavily. 'I could go in late.'

'That isn't enough.' She sat down opposite him and met his eyes challengingly. 'They need you. I've had their headmaster on the phone. He wants to see you as soon as you can make it.'

He closed his eyes and his mouth hardened to a grim line. 'Poppy, I can't deal with this tonight.'

'Well, you have to—you can't just ignore them and hope they'll go away!'

He opened his eyes and looked at her steadily. 'Can you deal with it, please? That's what you're here for.'

'No, it isn't!' she persisted. 'Damn it, you're their father, and there are some things only you can do. That's one of them. They need your time—'

The phone rang and Poppy answered it, then covered the receiver and turned to him.

'It's Mike,' she told him.

James sighed, picked up his Scotch and headed for the door. 'I'll take it in the library,' he said tiredly.

Poppy watched him go, then shrugged. What more could she say? She waited till she heard his voice on the other end, then hung up the phone. Dispirited, sorry for the boys, sad for James, she made herself a drink and went up to her flat.

Some time later she heard a noise from the children's room, and padded noiselessly across the landing in her bare feet.

James was standing in their doorway, one arm hitched up against the doorframe, defeat written in every line of his body.

He must have sensed her, because he turned round and met her worried eyes.

'Come and have a drink in my flat,' she urged quietly.

He turned back to the boys for a moment, then followed her, his footsteps surprisingly light.

She put the kettle on and went back into the sitting

room. He was studying her photos, picking them up and putting them down.

'You look as if you've had a happy childhood.'

'I have—I've been very lucky.'

He laughed mirthlessly. 'Damn it, Poppy, I've tried so hard to give them security in case anything should happen to me, and at the same time keep the home fires burning somehow.' He closed his eyes and shook his head slowly. 'I don't know how much longer I can go on.'

She didn't hesitate. Without thinking about it, she crossed the room, wrapped her arms round him and hugged him.

He stiffened for a second, then his arms came up and wrapped around her shoulders, holding her hard against his chest.

It felt so good! Her hands subconsciously absorbed the feel of him, the warmth, the solid columns of muscle each side of his spine, the way his waist tapered and the slight flare of his hips.

Her breasts were pressing against the solid wall of his chest, and his long arms felt curiously protective curving round her back.

A safe haven—that was what it felt like.

At least at first. Then from nowhere the tension sprang between them and he eased away from her, looking down at her with warm, questioning eyes.

She tipped her head back, searching his face. 'Are you OK?' she asked him, her voice echoing her concern.

'I'll live. Do you know how long it is since anyone gave me a simple, uncomplicated hug?' he asked gruffly.

Poppy felt her eyes fill. Releasing him, she turned away, unready to let him see how much he affected her.

There had been nothing uncomplicated about that hug—nothing at all!

'Would you like a cup of tea?' Damn, her voice was unsteady.

'I think not. I could do with going to bed.' He paused by the door, his eyes locked with hers. 'You're a wonderful woman,' he said quietly. 'Thank God we've got you. Goodnight, Mary Poppins.'

Then he left her, and she made her way to bed, turned out the light and buried her head under the covers so he wouldn't hear her crying for two small children and a lonely man who had lost his way.

'Is Dad back?'

Poppy looked up. William was standing in the kitchen doorway, pyjamas halfway up his legs where he had grown, eyeing her thoughtfully.

She nodded. 'He got back late last night.'

'He didn't come and see us.' His voice was truculent.

'You were asleep—he did go into your room, but he didn't want to wake you.'

William sat down at the table and kicked the chair-leg disconsolately with his bare toes.

She resisted the urge to hug him. Just then he would probably have thumped her. 'What do you want for breakfast?'

'Nothing.'

Unable to resist the unhappiness on his face any longer, Poppy sat beside him and laid her hand comfortingly on his arm. 'You ought to have something.'

He shrugged her hand off. 'Ice-cream.'

'William, don't be ridiculous,' she said gently but firmly. 'Have a piece of toast, or some cereal or something.'

'I don't want toast or cereal,' he yelled, suddenly losing his grip and jumping up. 'I want ice-cream!'

'Well, you can't have ice-cream,' she repeated firmly. Out of the corner of her eye she saw James emerge from the library and head towards the kitchen.

'Here's—'

'I *want* ice-cream, and if I can't have ice-cream, I don't want anything!' he screamed, tears forming in his eyes, and, turning towards the door, he pushed past his father and ran for the stairs.

'Obnoxious brat—'

'Mr Carmichael, leave him. He's upset.'

'I'll give him upset—George! George, come back here and apologise at once!' James bellowed after him.

Oh-oh, Poppy thought. This is going to cause havoc.

'George!'

The boy stopped and turned back towards his father.

'I'm not George,' he said clearly. 'I'm William—and if you were ever here, you'd know that!'

James stared after him in horror. 'Oh, my God,' he muttered, watching aghast as his son ran up the stairs and disappeared. In the distance a door slammed. He glanced at his watch. 'Poppy, calm him down, could you? I have to go out and I'm already late.'

'You can't! You can't possibly go out without talking to him first!'

He turned to meet the reproach in her eyes, and flinched.

'I'm sorry,' he said heavily.

'Don't apologise to me—it isn't me you've hurt. For God's sake, he's your son and you didn't recognise him!'

'From the back, running full-tilt—'

'Is it the first time?'

He was silent, his face grave, and a muscle worked in his jaw.

'James, please—'

'Poppy, I haven't time for this. I've got a meeting in half an hour and I have to sort out some notes—'

'You were going in late,' she said accusingly.

'That was before Mike arranged this meeting yesterday.'

'So delay it.'

'I can't—Poppy, don't do this to me. I'll be back later—I'll talk to him then.'

She shook her head sadly. 'You know, last night I really thought we were making some progress, but it's all just water off a duck's back, isn't it? Your business comes first, then the boys—a very poor second. For heaven's sake, James, you're all they've got!'

For a moment she thought she was going to win, but then he turned on his heel, picked up his briefcase and walked out of the front door, slamming it behind him.

'Well, damn you, James Carmichael!' Poppy muttered under her breath, and, taking the stairs two at a time, she ran up to the boys' bedroom.

William was face-down on the bed, sobbing as if his heart would break, and George was sitting next to him, patting him helplessly and swallowing hard.

'I hate him,' William hiccuped. 'He's mean and horrid and I hate him!'

'Oh, darling…'

Poppy scooped William up into her arms, gathered George in on the other side and rocked them gently until the storm died away.

'Don't be angry with him—he's working very hard at the moment, and he's awfully tired.'

'He's always tired—he always works hard. He's never

here, and when he is he shuts himself in the library and won't come out.' George's voice was full of bitterness.

'I wish he'd died instead of Mummy,' William said then, and Poppy could have wept for them.

James came back later, showered and changed and went out again for his dinner date with Helen.

He didn't have time to talk to the boys, and said he'd do so in the morning.

Poppy didn't hold out any great hope.

She and the boys had supper quietly in the kitchen. They were all subdued, and after they'd finished Poppy suggested they should go in the sitting room and watch the television.

But there was nothing on that appealed to them.

'We could look at the pictures,' William suggested.

'Pictures?'

'Of Mummy. Daddy won't let us get them out because he thinks it upsets us, but we think it upsets him. Anyway, he doesn't like it if we look at them when he's around—would you like to see her?'

'Yes, William, I think I would.'

He slid off the settee and ran to the bookcase in the corner, pulling out two photograph albums.

The first one was a wedding album, with their names embossed in silver on the cover. 'James Robert Carmichael and Clare Louise Thompson,' Poppy read.

She opened it and was confronted by a laughing, pretty girl with sparkling eyes and dark brown hair, and beside her a younger James, his arm possessively round his bride, his eyes alive and full of love and happiness.

'She was very pretty,' Poppy said to the boys. They nodded and turned the pages, introducing her in turn to all the various members of the family, but Poppy had eyes only for James, his eyes filled with pride, and Clare, small and pretty, bubbling over with joy.

She wondered how someone so full of life had died so tragically young. Perhaps the next album would give some clues.

But it didn't. There were more early photos, obviously taken on their honeymoon, and then baby photos of the boys, growing to toddlers, then to busy little terrors with wicked smiles and grubby knees.

Then, abruptly, there was nothing.

'She died that summer,' George told her. 'We don't go to the cottage any more.'

'Cottage?'

'In north Norfolk. It's on the clifftop. We can't remember going, but it's in lots of the photographs.'

'Is it your father's?' Poppy asked them.

William nodded. 'We asked Dad why we don't go any more, but he just says he's too busy.'

'The Frisbee goes, though, and lots of other people from work. It's just us that doesn't.'

'The Frisbee?'

William wrinkled his nose. 'Helen Fosby-Lee. We call her the Frisbee. She's dire!' He rolled his eyes. 'I mean, if you have an itch you ought to scratch it, but with that?'

Poppy bit her cheeks and struggled not to laugh. Where on earth had they heard that? Because there was no doubt about it, it was regurgitated parrot-fashion.

She scolded them gently for repeating things they didn't understand, and then chivvied them up to bed via the bath, ignoring their protests.

So he was scratching his itch with Helen, was he? she thought later as she tidied up the sitting room. Well, she supposed he was entitled. Why should the man live like a monk?

She was annoyed, though, that after the upset this morning he had gone out with his mistress rather than talk to his sons.

She decided it was time for a confrontation, and, curling up on the settee, she turned on the television with the remote control and channel-hopped her way through the evening.

He came back at midnight, just as the old grandfather clock in the hall was striking twelve.

'Hello, Cinderella,' she said to him, and he gave her a weary smile.

'Hello, Mary Poppins. You're up late.'

'Yes—I wanted to talk to you.'

He groaned. 'Can I get myself a drink? I'm stone-cold sober, bloody tired and harassed to death, but I don't suppose you're going to give up till you've had your say.'

He went over to the drinks cabinet in the corner and poured himself a hefty Scotch.

'OK, fire away.'

Poppy shrugged slightly. 'It's the boys,' she began.

He snorted. 'What else?' He threw himself down at the other end of the settee and watched her struggle for words. 'OK, come on, Poppy, hit me with it. What's been going on?'

She took a deep breath, let it out on a sigh and met his eyes. 'Do you ever talk to them about their mother?'

'Clare?' He sounded surprised. 'Not very often—but then, as you'll no doubt point out to me fairly soon, that probably isn't surprising.'

She lifted her shoulders helplessly. 'They say you're never here, you don't care, you won't let them look at pictures of their mother, you won't take them on holiday to the cottage, and—' She broke off, shaking her head.

He watched her. 'And?' he prompted gently.

'He probably didn't mean it—it was just said in the heat of the moment.'

'Who didn't mean what, Poppy? Tell me.'

She lifted her shoulders helplessly and met his eyes, her own filled with sorrow. 'William said he wished it had been you and not your wife.'

Pain clouded his eyes and he closed them briefly, shutting Poppy out. When he opened them again, they were shuttered and remote.

'On that, at least, we're in agreement. However, perhaps fortunately, things like that are beyond our control.' He drained his Scotch and refilled the glass. 'Drink?'

She shook her head. 'Did you have to go out tonight?'

'Yes—it was a business dinner, set up weeks ago. We were entertaining a foreign buyer. Fortunately he left early.'

'We?'

'Helen—she's my Corporate Affairs Director. She handles the PR and contract side of the business.'

Corporate affairs. How appropriate, Poppy thought uncharitably. 'The boys aren't very keen on her, I think.'

He laughed mirthlessly. 'I believe it's mutual. The last time she was here, they let her tyres down.'

Poppy stifled the grin, but not quickly enough.

He quirked a brow, and then his eyes twinkled. 'She was furious.'

'I'll bet. Who pumped them up?'

'The boys. It took them hours. I lent her my car.'

Poppy chuckled.

'Look, about tomorrow,' he said.

'Mmm?'

'I'll try and spend the day at home, but we've just taken over another company and we're having to rationalise it and turn it around. It's in a hell of a mess, but we're getting there. It just needs a bit more time.'

'On a Sunday?'

He sighed. 'As soon as possible, really. There are a lot of families who'll be affected unless we can get the company back on its feet and soon.'

He loosened his tie and leant his head back, rolling it towards her as he spoke.

'Buy me time, Poppy. Keep the kids in one piece while I get through this rough patch. It won't be long—two, maybe three weeks—then we can spend some time together.'

'Unless something else crops up.'

'It won't—I won't let it.'

His face was sincere, his eyes troubled, and his voice held conviction. He looked like a politician on the eve of an election, Poppy thought. She wished she could believe him.

CHAPTER THREE

THE boys were up early on Sunday morning, and they sat in the kitchen with Poppy, planning the day.

'We could go for a walk in the woods—would you like to do that?' she suggested.

'With Dad?'

She hesitated. Would it be better to say nothing, for fear of disappointing them?

'He did say he'd try and spend some time with you today.'

'Humph,' George said eloquently. 'He'll find something else to do.'

'He' strolled out of the library then, and smiled cheerfully at them. 'Morning, boys—morning, Poppy.'

She looked up and her heart sank. James was wearing his suit trousers, a shirt and a tie. I knew it, she thought.

He hitched up a chair and sat down with them. 'So, what are we doing today?'

Poppy eyed him sceptically. 'We,' she said with slight emphasis, 'were considering taking a walk in the woods behind the house. What are you doing?'

'Sounds good. I think I'll join you.'

'Great!' the boys yelled, and ran to get ready.

'Tell me something,' Poppy said casually. 'Do you sleep in your suit?'

He glanced down, as if surprised. 'I have to go into the office later. I thought it would save changing.'

Poppy suppressed a smile. 'I doubt it. It's awfully muddy out there. Haven't you got any jeans?'

44

He looked astonished, as if the idea of mud in early February hadn't even occurred to him. 'Somewhere, I think—maybe. I'll go and look.'

Five minutes later he was back, and Poppy instantly regretted sending him off to change. The jeans were old and soft, hugging his body with a familiarity that made her breath lodge in her throat. He had changed his shirt, too, putting on a dark polo-neck that clung to his chest and showed off his board-flat stomach to perfection, and he'd knotted a soft cream cable-knit sweater loosely round his shoulders.

He looked about ten years younger and rippling with raw, untamed masculinity, like a big cat in his prime, and Poppy felt suddenly terribly feminine and defenceless, desperately aware of the fact that they were almost alone in the house.

'Better?' he asked her.

Better? It was far, far worse, but she could hardly say that. Damn her hormones, anyway.

She mumbled something incoherent and turned away.

He followed her, catching her chin with his long, blunt finger and turning it towards him.

'Now what have I done?' he asked softly.

She met his eyes, her own wide and expressive, and suddenly the heat was flaring between them. He opened his mouth to say something, but the boys tumbled into the room excitedly and grabbed him by the arms.

'Come on, Dad! Let's go.'

Poppy dragged her eyes away from his and took a deep breath. 'Good idea,' she muttered, and pulled on her wellies and coat.

The boys tumbled out into the garden like puppies, rushing down towards the gate at the end that led to the woods.

James and Poppy followed more sedately, a careful distance between them. OK, so he'd said she was safe. Fine. So he wouldn't attack her. But then on the other hand the man wasn't fool enough to turn down what was offered him on a plate, and she was doing a fair job of that at the moment. She shoved her hands deep into her coat pockets, shrugged down inside the collar and tried to ignore him striding along beside her.

It was a gorgeous day, the sun breaking through the gaps in the trees and sparkling on the light frost that covered the ground.

Their breath misted on the cold air, and the boys ran ahead, laughing and chasing and playing tag.

'You're still mad with me, aren't you?' he said suddenly.

'No. No, I'm not mad with you. You're here, aren't you? That's what I asked for.'

'Yes, you did, didn't you? I wonder, was it just for the boys?' He stopped and turned her towards him. Their eyes meshed again, the message in his loud and clear. Poppy hoped her own were less expressive.

His hands came up to cup her shoulders, easing her gently towards him. They were so close that their breath mingled in a soft cloud between them, hanging in the still air. Oh, Lord, he was going to kiss her, she knew it, and any minute now her legs would give way and she would collapse in an undignified heap.

'Poppy...'

'Dad! Dad, come and see, there's a rabbit hole!'

He groaned and dropped his hands to his sides. 'Coming,' he called, and, casting her a look that smouldered with promise, he loped off along the path.

Poppy found a convenient fallen tree and sat down abruptly. What on earth was going on here? She'd been kissed before—heavens, she hadn't even *been* kissed by James, and she was carrying on like some fainting Victorian virgin with a fit of the vapours!

Well, she'd just have to make sure it didn't happen, because once it did she'd have no defences against him, and the boys needed her.

Let him scratch his itch with Helen, she thought ruthlessly, and felt a sudden, shocking stab of jealousy that ripped through her like a bullet.

'Indigestion,' she said aloud, and, pushing herself to her feet, she made herself go and join them.

James was watching her, his eyes following her every move, but she ignored him and talked to the boys, joining in their games with an excess of enthusiasm that brought a knowing smile to his lips.

'Avoiding me, Poppy?' he asked on the way back in, when they were alone for a second in the kitchen.

'Of course not,' she said briskly. 'What are your plans for the rest of the day?'

He chuckled. 'Trying to get rid of me? I thought you wanted me here?'

She gave a sharp sigh and turned to face him. 'Don't play games with me, Mr Carmichael. I'm here for the boys, not for your entertainment.'

His mouth hardened and he stepped back. 'I beg your pardon, Miss Taylor,' he said coldly. 'I'll be here for lunch, then in the office for the remainder of the day.'

She swallowed the hurt and turned away. It was for the best.

'Fine. I'll just go and change and then I'll start cooking.'

She tossed her head back, flinging her hair over her shoulder, and walked away, head held high. To hell with him, anyway. Arrogant beast. Why should she want him to kiss her? The next thing was he'd be suggesting an affair...oh, Lord. Her heart lurched against her ribs.

Oh, no. No way. Anyway, he had Helen. He was just playing with her, like a cat with a mouse.

It was a curiously painful thought.

Poppy lay in bed that night and tried to analyse her feelings for James Carmichael.

Physical desire, certainly. He was a very attractive man, and he had a charismatic appeal that went beyond his looks, but that was just hormones. Continuation of the species. Sex.

She felt heat lick along her veins, and fidgeted restlessly.

How could she feel that way for a man who neglected his children so badly?

Be fair, a little voice coaxed. He doesn't neglect them out of malice or ignorance, just circumstances, and he was doing his best to alter the circumstances—now. A little smile touched her lips. Poor man, she really must stop lecturing him and using emotional blackmail to get his co-operation. What he needed was support, not condemnation!

So, all right, she was attracted to him despite his failings. The fact remained she could never love a man who would allow his work to interfere with his relationship with his children—and, anyway, who was talking about love? She was just a temporary diversion, a little light relief in a hectic world that gave him no respite.

Except, of course, for Helen.

Poppy found it most odd that she could feel such jealousy and animosity towards a woman she had never even met, but she did. She wondered how serious their relationship was, because if he was considering marrying her, the boys would undoubtedly be most unhappy about it.

'Don't be absurd,' she chided herself. 'Maybe they just resent her because she isn't their mother. You haven't even met her yet. She might be really very kind.'

Somehow that made it worse. She bashed the pillow, turned over and counted sheep—then goats, then ducks... Finally she sat up and read until nearly four, and woke up at six-thirty with a crick in her neck where she'd fallen asleep sitting up.

James had left the house by the time she got downstairs just after seven. She was glad. After the tension yesterday she really didn't want to be alone with him any more than she had to.

The boys delivered safely to school, she returned to find the cleaning lady, Mrs Cripps, vacuuming noisily in the little sitting room. She had had the whole of last week off as well, and this was the first time Poppy had met her.

She approached her with an air of humility, as befitted a new arrival. The last thing she needed was to get on this lady's wrong side!

'Hello!' she said loudly over the ghastly din. 'I'm Poppy, the new nanny—and you must be Mrs Cripps.'

Mrs Cripps switched off the machine. 'Thought he must have got another one,' she said in the sudden silence. 'The mess isn't as bad as usual.' She was short and fat, her body encased in a cotton pinny, and she ran a jaundiced eye over Poppy. 'Hope you're better'n the last—she left pregnant. Got no more'n she deserved, I suppose. Morals of an alley-cat.'

She ran her eye over Poppy again, and sniffed. 'Easy to see why he chose you, though. Mind you don't fall into the same trap. But then perhaps you'll have more sense. Don't envy you, though—them kids is hell, poor little mites, drive me to distraction in the holidays, but you look as if you could cope. Don't let them drive you away—I don't think I could stand another holiday looking after them mornings.'

Poppy smiled faintly. 'I can cope with the boys, Mrs Cripps.'

'We'll see.' She sniffed again, and turned the vacuum cleaner back on. Poppy, thus dismissed, went smiling into the kitchen, shut the door and set about making a casserole for supper.

So the last nanny had left pregnant. But what had Mrs Cripps meant about James choosing *her*? Surely she didn't mean—oh, God. Poppy sat down with a plonk, and shut her eyes. Well, it wasn't unheard of. Plenty of married men diverted themselves with the nanny or au pair, God knows, and James wasn't even married any more, except to his job. Perhaps Helen was simply a colleague—perhaps he wasn't having an affair with her after all, and reserved his attentions for the nannies?

Poppy felt sick. She really didn't want to be the object of a music hall joke. Cross with herself for indulging in fantasies over him, angry with him for leading her on and flirting with her, she attacked the hapless vegetables and hacked up the chicken with a vengeance.

It was a good job he wasn't there, she thought with a humourless laugh, she probably would have dismembered him too.

Shortly afterwards the phone rang. It was the boys' headmaster, virtually demanding an interview with their father.

'Look,' Poppy said soothingly, 'why don't you give me a list of suitable times and I'll try and see what I can do—'

'Two-thirty or four.'

Poppy blinked. 'Today? What about tomorrow——?'

'No! Either he comes today, or the boys will be suspended.'

Poppy groaned quietly.

'All right, Mr Jones, I'll do what I can.'

She rang James's office, and asked to speak to him.

'He's in a meeting,' she was told.

'So get him out. This is important.'

'He said no interruptions, Miss——er——?'

'Taylor. Get him.'

'Really, it's more than my job's worth——'

Poppy was at the end of her tether. 'If you don't get him now, you won't have a job to worry about! Tell him the boys are in hospital.'

He was on the line in seconds. 'Poppy? What's happened?'

'Nothing, the boys are fine. I just needed to speak to you urgently and your guard dog wouldn't put me through.'

She could hear the rage and anxiety pouring down the telephone lines. 'Damn it, Poppy, don't ever do that again!' he bellowed. 'I nearly had a heart attack!'

She felt a pang of remorse. 'I'm sorry, but I had to talk to you. The school rang me.'

He groaned. 'Now what?' he said eventually.

'The headmaster is demanding an audience with you today.'

'I can't——'

'I don't think you have a choice. Either you see him, or he's suspending them. You can have two-thirty or four.'

There was a sharp sigh from the other end. 'Right,

make it four. We're going to run over tonight as it is, so God knows what time I'll get home.'

He hung up with a vengeance, and Poppy rubbed her ear and called the headmaster.

The boys looked subdued but rebellious when she picked them up from school. Eyeing them in the rear-view mirror, she thought she'd wait until they were settled at home before trying to get to the bottom of today's fiasco.

William broached the subject first, as they were sitting down in the kitchen with a glass of apple juice and a biscuit.

'He's going to see Dad, isn't he?'

'Mr Jones? Yes, he is. I gather you wrote something unkind about one of the children on the blackboard.'

George shrugged. 'Lucy started it—said she didn't believe Mummy was dead. She said she'd probably run away and left us because we were so horrid.'

'Oh, dear.' Poppy looked from one to the other. 'And why might she think you were horrid?'

William suddenly became terribly interested in the biscuit crumbs on the table.

'William?'

'I put a spider in her milk,' he blurted out. 'But she already told on me about the Maths test—'

'Maths test?' Poppy felt she'd fallen down a hole here. 'What Maths test?'

He kicked the table-leg. 'I didn't know the answers, so George helped me. It isn't my fault; I was sick when we did it before. She screamed.'

Poppy was getting muddled. 'Who screamed?'

'Lucy, when she saw the spider. She'd drunk half of it.'

'The spider?'

'No, silly, the milk. You can't drink spiders, the legs get all tangled—'

'OK, boys, that's enough. Right, I think we should get this homework done, and then I think a bath and hair-wash before supper, and an early night.'

'Aren't you going to punish us?'

Poppy resisted the urge to hug the little horrors. 'I think your father will probably want to discuss it with you when he sees you. In the meantime, let's get on, eh?'

James was predictably furious, but then he'd had the headmaster to deal with. By the time Poppy had filled him in on the background he was a little calmer, but still not really ready to see the funny side.

'I don't know how you can smile,' he said wearily. 'They really are getting beyond a joke.'

'They just need time.'

He snorted. 'Don't we all? And, talking of time, Helen's coming over this evening so we can carry on from this afternoon. I don't suppose you could find us something to eat?'

'I've done chicken marengo—will that be all right?'

'If it's what I can smell, it'll be fantastic. Bless you, Poppy. Where are the boys?'

'In bed, reading. Mr Carmichael?'

He arched a brow.

'Don't be too hard on them. They're just attention-seeking. Give them a cuddle and tell them not to do it again.'

His mouth lifted in a wry smile. 'I wasn't going to hit them, Poppy.'

'You don't have to hit them to hurt them. They're desperate for your approval. Just tell them you love them—they need to know that.'

A muscle worked in his jaw. 'You're good at this, aren't you? It's called emotional blackmail.'

Her mouth lifted slightly. 'I'm sorry, but someone has to be on their side.'

'It's all right, Poppy, I understand. I won't murder them—this time. And I'm on their side, too, you know. I'm just not very good at it.'

Poppy watched him go. For the first time she felt some hope for his relationship with the boys.

There was a scrunch of gravel, and James leant over the banisters.

'That'll be Helen—let her in and give her a drink, could you, Poppy? I'll be down shortly.'

So. At last she would meet the fabled Frisbee in person. Poppy drew herself up, took a deep breath and opened the front door.

Well, she was certainly beautiful, Poppy acknowledged fairly. About James's age, tall, slender, immaculately dressed in a smart pale grey suit and high heels, her blouse crisp and fresh, her make-up perfect, her hair smoothly wound into a bun—unlike Poppy's hair, that couldn't hold a kink and was even now slithering out of the ponytail band. At least, Poppy thought with a glimmer of satisfaction, her hair colour was her own, unlike the bottled streaks in Helen's carefully contrived honey-blonde...

Even so she felt distinctly underdressed in her old jeans and jumper, but horses for courses, and she'd like to see Helen after bathtime with the boys!

The lady in question—and there was no question that she was a lady, from the tips of her immaculately manicured fingers to the toes of her Italian leather shoes—slammed the door of her dark grey BMW and walked towards Poppy, eyeing her assessingly.

At the bottom of the steps leading to the front door she stopped, undaunted by Poppy's superior position at the top of the steps, and gave her a rather chilly smile that didn't reach anywhere near those icy blue eyes.

'You must be Poppy.'

Poppy smiled back guardedly. 'That's right—and you're Ms Fosby-Lee. We spoke on the phone. Do come in. Mr Carmichael is just putting the boys to bed; he'll be down in a minute. Can I get you a drink?'

Helen mounted the steps gracefully and handed Poppy her briefcase.

'Thank you. Put that in the library for me, would you, my dear? I must just go and freshen up—then perhaps a glass of dry white wine?'

Poppy gritted her teeth.

'Of course. Do you know where the cloakroom is?'

Helen gave a tinkling little laugh. 'Rather better than you do, I imagine. I'm hardly a stranger to the house.' She looked Poppy up and down. 'James is very taken with you, my dear. I must say he's been incredibly fortunate—reliable domestic staff are so hard to find these days.'

Poppy raised an eyebrow just the merest fraction. 'Really? We've never found that—but then we've had the same people for years. We don't seem to have any trouble keeping them, so we don't have to look for them very often.'

She smiled sweetly. Helen, bereft of a satisfactory answer and not at all sure if she actually *had* been insulted or not, turned on her heel and stalked off to the cloakroom.

Poppy watched her go with satisfaction, and debated putting some syrup of figs in her drink. Unfortunately it would be rather easily detected in white wine. Pity she wasn't having port.

She dumped the briefcase in the library, opened a well-chilled bottle of Chablis and poured a glass, taking it through to the library and setting it down on the desk.

'Domestic staff, indeed!' she muttered.

Then she went back to the kitchen and peered dispiritedly into the pot of chicken marengo. There was enough for two generous portions—not surprisingly, because that was what she had planned on catering for. Oh, well. She could have a cheese sandwich and a cup of coffee in her flat.

With a heavy sigh she measured out the wild rice and threw it in a pan of boiling water, then topped and tailed the fresh thin green beans. Damn Helen. This was her favourite meal.

James came down and found her muttering into the cutlery drawer.

She slammed it shut. 'OK?'

'Not really.' He gave a weary sigh. 'I need to talk to you later. They've got some idea in their heads that Clare died because of something they did wrong. I've tried to reason with them—I don't know, maybe I've got somewhere. Where's Helen?'

'Freshening up. James, don't worry. They'll be all right.'

She met his eyes and felt guilty for doubting the depth of his feeling for the boys. He tried to smile, but it was too much effort, and he closed his eyes and ran a hand tiredly over his face.

'Oh, Poppy, I wish I had your faith.'

She put a hand on his arm, seeking to comfort him. 'Don't worry,' she repeated softly. 'We'll get there.'

He opened his eyes then, and looked at her searchingly. 'I hope so—God, I hope so.'

His eyes dropped to her lips, then flicked back up to trap her in the flames of green and gold that burned in their depths. Poppy was mesmerised, drawn like a moth to the flame.

His lips parted on her name and she leaned towards him, her eyes wide with need.

'So this is where you've all got to!'

They leapt apart guiltily.

'Helen—sorry I wasn't around when you got here. Can I get you a drink?'

Her eyes moved from James to Poppy and back, knowledge burning in their ice-blue depths. She slipped her arm possessively through James's, and looked up at him through her lashes. 'Well, I did ask Poppy—'

'It's in the library. I opened the Chablis. Would you like a glass, James? I put the bottle back in the fridge.'

'That would be lovely—don't worry, I'll get it.' He opened the fridge and took the bottle out, gesturing to her with it. 'Poppy?'

'No, thank you. It's a little early for me.'

'I'll take the bottle, then. What time will supper be ready?'

'Any minute—where would you like it?'

'Have you eaten?'

'Yes,' she lied smoothly, 'I ate with the boys earlier.' Not for anything would she give that woman the satisfaction of knowing that she'd given up her supper for her!

'Oh, well, in that case, perhaps we'll take it through to the library and have it while we work. Give me a shout when it's ready and I'll come and get it.'

He ushered Helen out, and left Poppy in a fulminating silence in the kitchen.

She dished up the casserole, laid the things on a tray and took it through to the library.

'There's no need for you to wait on us—thank you, Poppy,' James said, his eyes warmly appreciative. She smiled.

'You're welcome. There's some sorbet in the freezer, and cheese in the fridge. I'm going up to my flat now.'

'OK, thanks. Goodnight, Poppy.'

'Oh, Poppy, before you go, I wonder if you could find me a little mineral water?' Helen asked with a sugary smile.

'Certainly, ma'am,' she said under her breath, and sketched a curtsey that Helen missed.

James, however, didn't, and followed her out.

'I'm sorry,' she said immediately. 'She's just...'

'Condescending?'

Poppy snorted inelegantly. 'She doesn't even bother to do that!' She shrugged helplessly. 'I'm sorry—I'm well aware that I'm your employee, but...'

Her shoulders lifted again, and dropped tiredly.

'You look shattered. Go to bed.'

'But you wanted to talk to me about the boys.'

'It'll keep. I'll look in later and see if you're still awake, but don't bother to wait up. This could take some time.'

'Wake me if you like.'

'OK.'

She turned towards the stairs and saw Helen standing in the doorway, listening. The woman's dainty, sharp little chin lifted with challenge, and Poppy smiled innocently. Had Helen heard her telling James to wake her? Probably. She wondered what she would make of it, and decided she didn't care.

'James is getting your mineral water—goodnight, Ms Fosby-Lee.'

Helen turned on her heel and stalked back into the library in silence. Poppy, stifling a chuckle, ran lightly up the stairs, humming softly.

All in all, she felt she'd won the first round.

She knew he was there, although he made no sound. She lay still for a moment, listening for the faint sound of his even breathing, then opened her eyes, wondering if she'd imagined it, but she hadn't. He was standing at the foot of the bed, silhouetted against the light, watching her.

She felt curiously vulnerable, knowing he had watched her while she slept. Her fingers curled defensively into the quilt, pulling it higher like a shield.

'I didn't mean to wake you,' he said softly.

'Sorry, I meant to stay awake, I know you wanted to talk to me. I'll get up—'

'No—no, stay there. The heating's gone off, you'll get cold.'

He lowered himself to the edge of the bed and watched her in silence as she sat up and pulled her dressing gown round her shoulders. Suddenly her perfectly respectable nightdress seemed flimsy and insubstantial under the lingering caress of his eyes.

'Has Helen gone?' she asked, to break the silence as much as anything.

'Yes, she went a few minutes ago. I'm sorry she was rude to you.'

'Oh, she wasn't rude,' Poppy said with characteristic fairness.

'Just bloody arrogant.' He smiled faintly. 'She can be a bit like that.' He moved nearer, his hand reaching out to touch hers where it lay on the bedspread.

He turned it over, tracing his finger along her life line. 'I wonder what life's got in store for you, Poppy?' he said quietly.

'Goodness knows—some bucolic young farmer, probably, and long hard hours raising endless pigs and sheep and children.'

She could see his mouth lifting with a smile.

'And will you like it?'

'I don't know—I'll tell you when I get there.' She hesitated for a second. 'How about you?'

'Work, work and more work—interspersed with difficult interviews with the boys' headmasters, I expect.' He gave a dry chuckle that covered a wealth of loneliness and despair. 'I can hardly wait.'

Her hand closed over his gently. 'Oh, James...'

He met her eyes, his own filled with longing. 'The nights are the worst, when I've worked myself to a standstill and still I can't sleep. It isn't even sex—if it was it would be easy to deal with. It's just someone to hold on to, to share the long hours with.' He reached out to her, his voice husky with emotion. 'Let me hold you, Poppy.'

It was beyond her to resist him. She lifted her arms, and he moved into them with a deep sigh, easing down on the bed beside her and enfolding her in a gentle embrace that demanded nothing.

There was no question of right or wrong; it felt completely natural to lie there in his arms, her ear against his chest, listening to the steady beating of his heart.

He lifted his head and studied her for a moment, then his hand came up and he threaded his fingers through her hair. 'So soft,' he murmured, and, bending his head, he laid his mouth gently against hers, his kiss a gift of infinite tenderness.

'Oh, Poppy,' he breathed, and then without warning the kiss changed, his mouth suddenly seeking, demanding, hard and hot and hungry, and Poppy felt her senses come alive in a wild surge of primitive passion.

She whimpered against his mouth and he muttered an apology, his tongue softly tracing the swollen outline of her lips.

They parted for him and his tongue delved gently, seeking out the soft velvet recesses, finding her tongue and teasing it with little flicks and tiny bites that made her moan with need.

His hand moved slowly across her shoulder to her throat, his fingertip teasing the hollow where her pulse beat like a wild thing under his touch, then it moved down, down, until it reached her breast, his palm chafing lightly against the straining peak.

The fine cotton lawn of her nightdress was no barrier to sensation, and she arched up, drawn tight as a bow-string by his teasing caress.

At last his large, firm hand closed gently over her breast, bringing instant relief, but it was short-lived, a fleeting balm in a wild torrent of desire that came from nowhere and threatened to swamp her.

She moaned his name against his lips, and he lifted his head, scattering hot, open-mouthed kisses down her throat, circling her nipple with devastating intent.

'Please—oh, please!' she begged, and then his mouth closed hotly over the aching peak, drawing it into his mouth and suckling it hard.

She cried out softly in the darkness and he shifted

against her, moving to share the pleasure equally with its eager twin.

Her fingers wound through his hair, soft and springy beneath her palms, cradling his head against her breasts as he drove her wild with his clever tongue.

He moved up over her again, his weight pressing her down into the mattress, his mouth seeking hers again in desperation. His breathing was ragged, and against her breasts the savage beating of his heart matched her own.

Even through the quilt she could feel the hard thrust of his arousal against her thighs, and her hands ached to touch him, to feel the hot satin of his skin beneath her palms.

Then suddenly, as suddenly as he had started, he stopped, dropping his head on her shoulder with a shaky sigh.

'What the bloody hell are we doing, Poppy?' he asked raggedly. 'I only meant to hold you...'

Sanity returned slowly, like the seeping cold of the winter ground, chilling her to her bones.

She could hear Mrs Cripps talking about the other nanny, and saying it was easy to see why he had chosen Poppy. She had fallen headlong into the trap.

She closed her eyes as a hot rush of shame flooded her cheeks.

'Please let me go,' she whispered unsteadily, and with a heavy sigh he lifted himself away from her and swung his legs over the bed, his hands hanging between his knees, his head bowed.

'I'm sorry,' he said quietly, and his voice sounded somehow distant. 'I promised you I wouldn't do that— forgive me. It won't happen again.'

She struggled to a sitting position and tugged the quilt

up round her chest, tucking it under her arms as if it could protect her from her shame.

'About the boys—' she began, her voice unsteady.

'Not tonight, Poppy,' he said gruffly. 'My control is hanging on by a thread. I think I'd better get out of here before I give in to the urge to tear that quilt off you and bury myself in your soft, willing body.'

He stood up, ran his hands through his hair and walked slowly from the room, leaving Poppy aching with need and burning with humiliation.

She was up before the rest of the house, dressed in a tracksuit and trainers, as sexless as possible. She cleaned the boys' shoes, laid the breakfast things and then slumped at the table with a cup of tea.

What a fool she'd been! But no more. Oh, no! From now on she was keeping him at arm's length, and her sympathy would very definitely be reserved for the boys. Damn her soft heart, anyway!

A door opened and closed and she looked up, that soft heart sinking as she saw James crossing the hall towards her. He was dressed in a suit, his hair still slightly damp from the shower, and he looked immaculate and remote.

'Good morning,' she said formally. 'There's tea in the pot.'

'Thank you.' He helped himself, pulled up a chair and sat down opposite her with a sigh. 'About last night...' She looked up and met his eyes, and saw the remoteness falter for a second. 'It won't happen again, Poppy—I promise.'

She stirred her tea to occupy her hands. 'I'd already decided that. I don't want to become another notch on your bedpost.' She laid the spoon down very precisely. 'About the boys—'

He sighed. 'Yes, the boys. I don't know what we can do. God knows where they got this idea from that Clare died because of them.'

'Do you ever talk to them about how she died?'

He sighed again. 'Probably not. I tend not to talk about it.'

'Is it still painful?'

'Painful?' He glanced quickly at her, then away. 'No, not really, not any more. It was very sudden, though, and I felt...'

He paused, and Poppy waited, giving him time. He picked up the pepper-grinder, inspecting it closely. 'She had a headache. She often had them, so it wasn't anything very unusual. We had to go out to a business dinner and she decided she couldn't go, so we cancelled the babysitter and she went to bed early. When I came in she was asleep, apparently quite normally, but she didn't seem to hear me come in. I had some paperwork to do, so I went back down to my study and worked till about four, then I went back up.'

He put the pepper-grinder down very carefully. 'She was dead. She'd had a brain haemorrhage—a weak blood vessel that had finally given up. She was twenty-seven; I wasn't quite thirty. You don't expect that sort of thing to happen when you're that age.

'The business was beginning to take off, and I threw myself into it so I didn't have to cope with my grief. I thought if I kept myself busy enough I wouldn't have time to think, but even if I worked till two and got up at six, there were still four hours with nothing but emptiness.'

He sighed and picked up the pepper again. 'After a while it stopped hurting, but then the loneliness really got under way.'

'And you carried on burying yourself in your work so you wouldn't have to deal with that, either.'

He met her eyes, and laughed ruefully. 'Pop psychology? Or should I say Poppy psychology?'

'Am I right?'

He sighed. 'Yes. You know you are. Now I'm trapped by it.'

She poured them both another cup of tea and sat down again. 'When I first met you, I thought you needed a miracle,' she said softly. 'But you don't, you need a wife.'

He inhaled sharply, then let his breath out on a long, denying sigh. 'No. Oh, I'll grant you the idea has appeal—a mother for my children, someone to keep the home fires burning, a warm and willing woman in my bed at night—but, just in case you've got any ideas about applying for the job, you can put it right out of your pretty, warm-hearted little head, because I don't have either the time or the inclination for another emotional commitment.'

She smiled understandingly. 'Not me. I'm going to marry a farmer, remember? But I think Helen has her eye on the post.'

'Helen?' His voice was incredulous. 'Don't be silly—she's a colleague, at most a friend, nothing more.'

'Then why was she jealous of me last night?'

His brows twitched together. 'She wasn't.'

'She was—why do you think she tried so hard to put me down? She saw me as a threat, James.'

'Rubbish!'

Poppy sighed softly. 'Suit yourself,' she told him, and put the cups in the sink. How could he *be* so naive?

CHAPTER FOUR

JAMES stuck to his promise. For the rest of that week Poppy hardly saw him at all, and when she did it was in the company of the boys. They were very wary of their father, but he was making a real effort to talk to them and to listen to their answers, and several times she found them together in the little sitting room, going through the photo albums and talking about Clare.

The downside of this was that he left the house at five every morning to get the hours in at the office, and Poppy could see him getting more and more tired with every day that passed.

And Helen didn't like it. 'I thought you had a nanny now for the children?' she overheard the woman say one evening, when she had come round after supper to go over some paperwork with James.

'I have.'

'So let her look after them.'

Poppy couldn't be bothered to listen to any more. The woman was so cold and hard and unfeeling she wondered James could bear to be in the room with her, never mind work with her day after day, week after week...

She took them coffee in the drawing room later, and couldn't help but notice how Helen matched the room. Poppy hated the room, so it was no surprise to her that Helen liked it so much.

Funny, she had the distinct feeling James hated it too. It was colourless—a mass of white and cream so tediously neutral that Poppy wanted to drag some pillarboxred cushions in there and fling them around just to liven things up!

The furniture was all new, limed ash in the same neutral tones as the upholstery and the doubtless hideously expensive ivory silk wallpaper, and the curtains were swagged and full and trailed artistically all over the colourless carpet.

Poppy tried to imagine the damage that would result from a wet, muddy collie running in off the farmyard and having a damn good shake in the middle of the floor, and it cheered her up no end.

She retreated to the kitchen, making herself a cup of cocoa and curling up by the boiler with a book. It wasn't quite the same as the Aga at home, but it came a pretty close second and she didn't fancy closeting herself in the flat.

Shortly before ten she heard James showing Helen out of the door, and she went through to the drawing room to retrieve the tray. James walked in behind her and helped, taking it from her and removing her temptation to drop the thing and watch the coffee pot savage the immaculate carpet—

'Poppy? What's wrong?'

She blinked. 'Wrong? Nothing.'

'You look ready to kill.'

She smiled faintly. 'I do?'

'You do. Want to talk about it?'

She sighed and shoved her hand through her hair, raking it up off her face and dropping it carelessly so it tumbled over her shoulders again. 'I just hate this room.'

His smile was wry. 'Do you? That's interesting. So do I.'

She looked at him in astonishment. 'You do? So why is it like this?'

His laugh was tinged with embarrassment. 'I had it done by a designer at huge expense.'

'Don't tell me—a friend of Helen's?'

'Yeouch. You really hate her, don't you?'

'Hate?' Poppy felt guilty. 'It's not my business to hate or like her.'

'That wasn't what I said.'

'No.' She shifted uncomfortably, but he let her off the hook.

'In answer to your question, yes, it was a friend of Helen's. She did Helen's flat, too.'

Poppy looked round the room. 'It's just so—'

'Colourless?'

She smiled. 'Yes. Absolutely. And new. In an old house, I would have thought you'd have antiques. You have everywhere else.'

'Yup.' His lips pursed thoughtfully. 'Helen—ah— thought it might be nice to have one room that was more contemporary. I hardly use it—it was worth a try.'

'And you hate it.'

His mouth quirked. 'I find it very—' he shrugged '— neutral.'

They shared a smile.

'So what would you do to it?' James asked her.

'Colour. I'd warm it up a bit—put some colour in the curtains—perhaps a contrast lining in the swags and tails—some coloured cushions, a nice carpet in the cen-tre—and I'd get rid of the limed ash and put some warm, old wood in here—mahogany, probably, or bird's eye maple. Maybe both.'

'Where from?'

She looked at him in astonishment. 'Auction sales.'

His mouth lifted. 'I haven't been to an auction sale for years. Not since Clare and I first got married.' He looked down at the tray in his hands, but not before Poppy caught a flash of sadness in his eyes.

Oh, hell, she thought. Well, perhaps it would do him good to remember the woman who had put that smile on his face in the photos. It might make him see the wretched Frisbee more clearly.

'How about cocoa?' she suggested.

James looked up at her again, his expression strangely expectant. 'Cocoa? In the kitchen?'

Poppy grinned. 'Or we could come in here?'

He gave a mock shudder, and the last trace of sadness faded from his eyes. 'Kitchen, I think,' he said with a grin, and Poppy followed him out, not even bothering to hide her smile. Five minutes later they were slouched over the table nursing steaming cocoa, and Poppy was idly trailing a spoon around in the froth at the top. She broke the companionable silence.

'So, how are you getting on with the children?' she asked him softly.

James sighed. 'OK. I didn't realise they were so obsessed with their mother. I thought they would hardly remember her, and of course I'm right, they only have a very sketchy memory. That's the trouble. They want to know everything about her, and only I can tell them.'

'What about Clare's parents?'

He shook his head. 'They can't talk about her. They've never really dealt with their grief, and they can't cope with seeing the boys.'

'How sad.'

James heaved a sigh. 'Yes. I think so. They need their grandparents. God knows, they've seen little enough of me.'

'But you're changing that.'

He met Poppy's eyes, his own sceptical. 'I'm trying.

But I really am busy at work, and, although I'd love to comply with your ideals, it doesn't necessarily pan out like that, Poppy. I'm not convinced it ever will.' He looked down at his cocoa, swirling the mug pensively.

'They treat me like a stranger, Poppy,' he said quietly. 'As if they don't know me.'

'And do they?'

He looked up at her, his eyes fathoms deep with sorrow. 'No. And I don't know them any more. They've changed—grown up, I suppose. Turned into people. When Clare died they weren't much more than babies, and their needs were so simple to meet. Food, shelter, affection—it was so much more straightforward. Now they want answers to difficult questions, questions I hardly know the answer to myself.'

He looked down again, and Poppy felt her eyes fill. 'James, you'll be all right,' she told him earnestly. 'You just need to do things together.'

'Like what? I don't even know what they'd like to do!'

Poppy shrugged. 'Go to the zoo? Perhaps you could do that this weekend?'

He looked horrified. 'The zoo? Good grief, Poppy, do you have any idea how long it is since I went to the zoo?'

She laughed. 'Twenty-five years?' she offered.

He snorted. 'Easily. Probably more. Anyway, this weekend's out. I have to go to Birmingham for a conference about this takeover.'

Poppy put her spoon down very deliberately and sat back in the chair. 'James, I don't want to be awkward, but I haven't had a day off in two weeks and it's the start of their half-term, so I'll be going flat out with them all next week! You can't go away this weekend—not unless someone else is having the children?'

He looked at her in blank astonishment. 'Someone else—no. Oh, hell, Poppy, I'm sorry. I just didn't think. I'll ask Mrs Cripps.'

'She'll say no.'

'Not if I offer her enough money.'

Poppy sighed. 'They hate her.'

He rammed his big hands through his hair, ruffling the tight curls and leaving them in chaos. Poppy longed to reach out and smooth them down again—

'What do you suggest, then?'

'Apart from a weekend off, which I take it is out of the question?'

He lifted his shoulders helplessly. 'I can't. I'm sorry, it's just not possible to reschedule it for any other time.'

'Can I take them home with me to the farm for the weekend? That way I get to have a break, and so do they.'

He looked as if she'd just offered him eternal life on a plate. 'What's the catch?' he asked.

Poppy laughed shortly. 'No catch. But they'll have to fit in with the others—get up early, help with the stock, go out on the farm with my brothers. They'll be quite safe—probably tired, but safe. My mother will feed them till their tummies burst, and they'll sleep like logs after all the fresh air.'

'It sounds wonderful—can I come?' he joked, but behind the words Poppy detected a real sense of longing. When had he last had fun? she wondered. Really let his hair down and enjoyed himself? She found herself trapped by his lovely hazel eyes, and without thinking she reached out a hand and laid it against the hard plane of his jaw. The skin was taut, scratchy with stubble this

late in the day. Her fingers were fascinated by it. She
dropped her hand before she did something silly, like
slide her fingers round behind his head and drag him
towards her for a kiss—

'You'd be more than welcome to join us if you could
get away,' she said softly.

His eyes creased with a smile that tipped one side of
his mouth in gentle irony. 'Thank you, Poppy. If there
were only enough hours in the day…'

Poppy spent the weekend wondering how he would have
fitted in, and she found herself somewhat confused. The
James she saw every day leaving for work or shut up in
the library at night would have been lost at the farm.
The man who had dressed in jeans and chased through
the woods with his sons would have had a whale of a
time.

But which man was the real James? 'Who is he,
Bridie?' she asked the beautiful but totally scatty Irish
setter that was draped across her lap. Bridie thumped her
tail and peered up at Poppy through her glorious auburn
eyebrows, her great liquid eyes adoring.

Poppy stroked her shoulder and sighed. 'I don't know
either,' she told the dog. 'I wish I did.'

'Know what?' her mother asked, coming into the
room behind Poppy.

'Who James is. He's so busy being Mr Big he doesn't
ever stop to be himself. I wonder if he even knows who
he is any more.'

Audrey Taylor settled herself on the floor beside
Poppy and reached across to scratch the dog's ears affectionately. 'Pity he couldn't come, too. It would do
him good to relax.'

Poppy gave a hollow laugh. 'Wouldn't it just! We

went for a walk in the woods the other day, and if I hadn't sent him to change he would have come in his suit trousers and a tie!'

Audrey chuckled, then gave Poppy a searching look. 'Tom was very worried, you know. Thought you were going to get into all sorts of trouble with him. Of course, I've never met him, and I trust your judgement, but I just wondered what it was exactly that made Tom's alarm bells ring.'

Poppy rolled her eyes. 'He thought James was too masculine, for heaven's sake!'

'And is he?'

A faint tide of warmth stained Poppy's cheeks. 'He's just a man, Mum. Just a lonely, unhappy man.'

Audrey looked at her daughter thoughtfully for a moment, then said, 'Hmm.'

'Hmm?'

'Perhaps Tom was right. Perhaps you are in trouble— but not the sort of trouble he meant.'

Poppy met her mother's gentle, searching gaze and bit her lip. 'I think you could well be right, Mum. I think you could well be right...'

The road was nearly empty. Mile after mile of lonely motorway and dual carriageway, with nothing to think about but the mess he had made of the boys' lives. Had he really failed them so badly?

Probably—and it had taken Poppy, with her wide eyes and generous heart, to show him. She was good for them, warm and friendly and accepting, but by no means a push-over. He'd been listening to their daily bustle, and it was quite clear from the routine conversations that they were trying it on and she was definitely not falling for it.

He wondered how they were getting on at the farm, and a wave of loneliness washed over him, catching him by surprise. A distant memory tugged at him, from back in his childhood, of staying with his uncle at a huge old vicarage in Hampshire and going with his cousins to the farm at the end of the long, rambling garden.

It had smelt of cows and pigs and chickens, and there had been an ancient pony they had patted, and sometimes the farmer would let them ride on the tractor. In the summer they had helped with the harvest—well, 'helped' was perhaps too strong a word, but they had spent many happy hours playing in the fields in the glorious summer sunshine.

Nostalgia brought a smile to James's mouth. They had been happy days—days before the reality of life had rammed home with such terrifying force. Before marriage, and responsibility, and the pressures of his business success—and before life had cruelly snatched his bride so long before her time, leaving him and the boys bereft of warmth and comfort.

Until Poppy.

There was a sign up ahead. Left was towards Norwich and home. Straight on a little further would take him almost to the Taylors' farm. He hesitated just a moment, then ignored the turn-off. God knows if he could find the farm; he only had the vaguest idea where it was. It was possible, too, that Poppy and the boys had already left, but he had a sudden, desperate urge to be with them, to forget his business problems and the endless convolutions of the takeover, and just take time out.

He turned off the main road towards the village where the farm was supposed to be, and resigned himself to spending hours cruising round the countryside in a fruitless search. He was lucky, though. By a fluke he found it easily, and turned into through the wide farmyard gate, pulling up outside the big pink Tudor house that he had seen in one of Poppy's photos.

It was nearly four, and in the house the lights blazed a welcome. For him? He opened the car door and hesitated.

It was years since James had been nervous about anything. In a boardroom he could cope with anything anyone threw at him. Here, now, at Poppy's home, he felt like a fish out of water. He almost drove away, but then the back door opened and a woman came out, familiar to him again from Poppy's photos. With a resigned sigh he got out of the car and walked over to her.

'Mrs Taylor?' he said, although he knew.

'Yes—and you must be James,' she said, and her smile enveloped him in warmth. 'Did you get away early?'

'Yes. I'm sorry to intrude, but Poppy painted such a wonderful picture—'

She cut him off with a wave of a floury hand. 'You aren't intruding at all. It's a pleasure to see you. Come into the kitchen and keep me company. I'm just finishing off a batch of scones while we wait for the boys to come back. Poppy's in the bath, grabbing a bit of peace and quiet while the going's good, and I'm making tea. You can butter the bread so you don't have to feel guilty.'

She led him into the warm, bright kitchen, showed him where to hang his suit jacket beside all the battered wax jackets and ancient anoraks on the row of hooks by the door, then sat him at the kitchen table in front of a mound of freshly cut bread.

'Tea?' she offered, heaving up the cover of the hot-plate and putting the big kettle on the Aga to boil.

'Thank you, that would be lovely.'

She bustled about, handing him a knife and the soft, fresh butter to spread on the bread. It looked suspiciously home-made, he thought, and sniffed appreciatively. Gorgeous. He rolled up his sleeves, spread and stacked and all but drooled.

'Have a bit.'

He met her eyes and gave a wry grin. 'Am I so easy to read?'

She chuckled. 'Let's just say I'm used to hungry boys. Go on.'

His smile widened. 'I think I will; it smells wonderful.'

He sank his teeth into it and the flavour burst on his tongue, making him groan with pleasure. 'Wow. After eating hotel food all weekend, this is...' He waved a hand, speechless.

'Poppy made it.'

'She's a talented girl.'

Mrs Taylor plonked a mug down in front of James and settled herself opposite with another mug. 'She is. She's also got a very soft heart.'

The warning was clear. James met her eyes, understanding the concern he saw in them. 'I know. Don't worry, Mrs Taylor, I won't hurt her—not in the way you mean. I'll annoy her and frustrate her to bits, I have no doubt, but on a personal level I—' He looked down at his tea, suddenly conscious of the ambivalence of his feelings.

'She's a very attractive girl. I know that. But she's safe with me. The boys need her in their lives too much for me to jeopardise their relationship with her for a fleeting one of my own. And, anyway, she deserves more than that, much more. I have too much respect for Poppy to use her as a temporary diversion.'

Audrey Taylor regarded him steadily over the table, then nodded briefly. 'You'll do,' she said cryptically, and stood up. 'Finish buttering the bread; they'll be in in a minute.'

As she turned her back, James heaved a silent sigh of relief. He was conscious of having passed a test, but which test and for what, he didn't have a clue. He wasn't sure he wanted to know! He buttered the bread, drank his tea and then washed up the mugs in the sink while Audrey bustled about laying the table and checking the scones.

While they worked he was vaguely aware of sploshing noises overhead, and a sudden image of Poppy in the bath made his breath catch and heat race along his veins. And just when he had told Mrs Taylor that Poppy was safe with him!

Safe, my aunt Fanny, he thought disparagingly to himself. Did she really believe him? She wouldn't if he carried on thinking about her daughter like this, because his body was all set to betray him if he couldn't drag his feeble mind off the image of her skin slick with soap, the firm swell of her breasts—

He almost groaned aloud. He was contemplating going out into the chilly February air without the benefit of a coat, to settle his libido down again, when the back door burst open and the boys erupted into the room, accompanied by Tom and a boy of about sixteen whom James took to be Poppy's youngest brother. Around their feet seethed a very wet and muddy dog.

'Dad!' one of the twins said, stopping dead in his tracks.

James looked carefully. 'Hello, George. William.'

He gave them a cautious smile, but they didn't smile back. Instead they eyed him suspiciously.

'Have you come to take us back?' William asked.

'No—well, not yet. Not before tea. Hello, Tom. Good to see you again.' He reached over the boys and the dog and shook Tom's hand, and then extended his hand to the other lad. 'James Carmichael—you must be Peter.'

The boy nodded, eyeing him assessingly just as Tom had done. The frank blue gaze was Poppy's own, and James found himself inspected yet again. He stifled a smile.

'So, boys, had a good time?' he asked the twins.

They nodded. 'Yes—great,' George said. 'We've just been out shooting. Bridie's useless.'

This last remark was made with such scorn that James blinked. 'Bridie?' he asked in confusion, his mind still paralysed with the thought of the boys shooting.

The dog, hearing her name, bounced up to him and lolled against his leg, spreading mud up his trouser-leg with a beseeching paw.

'Oh, Bridie, no!' Mrs Taylor cried, but James found his hand going down to fondle the dog's head.

'Don't worry. The suit needed cleaning.' Bridie licked his hand with great enthusiasm and beamed up at him, clearly besotted by someone with such excellent taste. He grinned despite himself and scratched her chin. 'You soppy dog.'

'The boys are right—she's a useless gun dog,' Tom said, shucking his coat and hanging it behind the door. 'She runs when the gun goes off. Here, Pete, put it away, could you?'

He handed the gun to his brother, and James was relieved to see it was broken and the cartridges had been removed. The thought of the boys let loose with a gun was enough to bring him out in a rash. The concern must have shown on his face, because he felt a hand on his arm.

'They've been quite safe, you know,' Audrey Taylor assured him. 'Our boys are very sensible with guns. We've made sure of that.'

'I'm relieved to hear it,' he muttered.

Then a door opened and closed behind him, and the hairs stood up on the back of his neck. He turned slowly, and as his eyes met Poppy's he felt his heart thud behind his ribs.

'Hi,' he said, suddenly self-conscious. Would she mind him invading her home?

No. A warm smile lit her eyes, and she crossed the room towards him. For a moment he thought she was going to hug him, but then she stopped short and raised her hands palm up in a gesture of amazement. 'Hi, yourself. You got away!' She looked pleased and surprised, and he had to forcibly stop himself from hugging her.

'Yes. I couldn't help myself; I could smell your bread cooking.'

'Liar.' She laughed, a soft, warm sound that curled round his heart and eased away the last remains of tension. He felt his mouth tilt in a smile, and was oblivious of the looks exchanged behind them. He was too busy looking at Poppy, her hair still wet from the bath, her face scrubbed clean, her eyes bright. Lord, she was lovely.

Only the crash of the back door signalling the arrival of Poppy's father stopped him from disgracing himself by pulling her into his arms and kissing her senseless.

They all turned, and yet again James found himself subjected to the scrutiny of a pair of cornflower-blue eyes. These eyes, however, were the eyes of a father, and it wouldn't have surprised James a bit to have been wheeled out into the hall, a hand firmly on his shoulder, and interrogated as to his intentions.

Instead the man held out a hand—cold, hard, work-roughened—and extended the same welcome as his wife, cautiously friendly. They gathered round the table and tucked into the biggest and most traditional high tea James had seen since his childhood, with heaps of lean home-cured ham, cold chicken and beef, a fresh crunchy winter salad, the bread he had buttered—and the most tempting array of cakes he had seen in his life.

He feared for the waistband of his trousers, but it was too delicious to turn away from. Finally he admitted defeat and sat back, to see Poppy watching him with an indulgent smile.

The others were still eating, the boys talking nineteen to the dozen, and Tom recounting the details of their disastrous afternoon with the scatty dog. James looked down at Bridie's head resting hopefully on his knee, and stroked her ears. 'Were you a bad girl?' he asked gently.

'Stupid—I don't know about bad,' Tom said in disgust. 'Cat food, Bridie, that's all you're fit for. Useless woman.'

Bridie yipped indignantly, and Poppy defended her, too.

'Sexist pig,' she said placidly. 'Don't know why you want to go out and shoot harmless things, anyway. Pass the bread, James.'

There followed an obviously well-worn wrangle, and James sat back and soaked it all up. An only child, he had never enjoyed the dubious benefit of squabbling with his siblings, and he found himself smiling at their silliness. He was subliminally conscious of Bridie moving away from his leg, and then suddenly, under cover

of the distraction, she reached up and swiped a big slice
of ham from the plate at the edge of the table.

'Bridie!' everybody yelled, and the dog shot under the
chair in the corner and swallowed the ham, then came
out wriggling, tail going furiously, an ingratiating grin
on her face. It was too much for James.

He started to chuckle, and the chuckle grew despite
his attempts to control it. He propped his elbow on the
table and put his hand across his mouth to smother the
mirth, but it would have none of it.

'It's not funny!' Poppy protested, glaring at the setter.
'She's a *bad dog*!'

Bridie wriggled up to James and rolled onto her back,
to howls of protest from the family, and he gave up.
Throwing back his head, he laughed until his sides ached
while the family remonstrated helplessly with the unre-
pentant hound. Then he straightened up, still chuckling,
and noticed the boys were watching him, their faces
shocked.

The laughter left him at a stroke. 'What's the matter?'
he asked worriedly.

'You were *laughing*,' George said.

'You don't *ever* laugh,' William added, his voice
hushed with awe.

There was a stunned silence at the table, and James
felt as if he'd been punched in the gut. Did he really
laugh so rarely that the boys were shocked that he had?

'He is allowed to, you know,' Poppy said gently,
breaking the silence, and then the boys looked at her
instead of him and the breath eased back into his lungs.
Oh God, he thought, have I really become such a mis-
ery? He tried to remember the last time he had laughed
with them, and he found he couldn't. He was dismayed,

and grateful to Poppy for distracting the boys while he recovered his composure.

He studied them, noting the glow in their cheeks and the light in their eyes. Bless Poppy for bringing them here. Obviously they'd loved it, and he realised suddenly that if he could have chosen an upbringing for them, this would have been it.

Sadness washed over him again—regret that he'd failed them, sorrow that Clare wasn't there to share their lives, despair that he might never be able to offer them the real ingredients of a home. He looked up to find Poppy watching him, her eyes concerned, and he dredged up a smile.

Her eyes softened, sending him a message of—what? Comfort? Promise? Promise of what, though? Happy ever after?

He knew better than that. He looked away, unable to cope with her understanding. Damn, he wanted her all of a sudden, despite his promise to her mother. Well, tough. He'd discovered self-discipline years before. He'd just have to exercise it.

They all finally finished eating and adjourned into the drawing room, a big room with a huge log fire and great squashy sofas, the riot of flowers smothering the curtains at each window echoed in the tapestry cushions that were dotted around the place. The floor was scattered with Persian carpets, and Bridie threw herself down on one in front of the fire and went instantly to sleep. James was tempted to join her. His eyelids could droop with very little encouragement.

'What a beautiful room,' he said to Audrey with a sigh.

'Isn't it? Poppy redid it for us last year and we're thrilled.'

He turned to Poppy at the other end of the big sofa. 'Can you do this to mine? Turn it into a home?'

Was the longing written so clearly in his eyes? He could have sworn he saw pity there in hers. 'I can try. I thought you were joking.'

He shook his head. 'No. Really. Could you try?'

She nodded. 'I'd have to go to some auctions for the furniture.'

He turned to Audrey, a wry smile on his lips. 'Is that safe, letting her loose with my money?'

She laughed. 'Depends how brave you are. She's no fool, but she's got a good eye. You may end up with a sizeable bill but your money would be well invested.'

He turned back to Poppy. 'I'm in your hands,' he said softly.

Something flared in her eyes, and found an echo in his veins. Their eyes locked, the message plain, and he forced himself to look away. Damn, this was going to be hard. Impossible.

It dawned on him then that keeping his promise to her mother would be one of the most difficult things he had ever done...

CHAPTER FIVE

JAMES was acting strangely.

For a moment, there, Poppy had thought things were actually improving. At her parents' house he had seemed relaxed and comfortable, and then suddenly—wallop. Different James. Distant again, but only with her.

With the boys he seemed better, more relaxed, and once or twice she even heard him laughing with them, as if having rediscovered his sense of humour he kept getting it out and playing with it like a new toy. The boys loved it, and he seemed to love it, too. Probably for the first time in years he was actually having fun—but not with her.

With her he was—well, nothing. He wasn't with her at all. That was the difference. Where before he had sought her out, now he seemed to avoid her, closeting himself in the library when a week ago he might have come and had a cup of coffee and watched her work in the kitchen, or helped load the dishwasher and then suggested a nightcap in the sitting room.

The only conversation they had was about the boys, or with the boys, and although it was silly, and she told herself so countless times a day, she missed him.

'Good job, too,' she told herself. 'You have no business hankering after the man. Concentrate on your job and leave him alone.'

But she couldn't help it. She found her thoughts straying to him umpteen times a day, and in between she was too busy with the boys to concentrate on anything else.

It was their half-term week, and she planned all sorts of activities. There was a gap, though, towards the end of the week, and on Thursday evening they were sitting down for supper—without James, as usual—and Poppy asked them what they would like to do the next day.

They shrugged. 'Dunno, really,' William said. 'It would be nice to do something with Dad.'

'Don't hold your breath,' George said sagely. He was the more pragmatic of the two, the more outward going and verbally direct. William was the thinker, the worrier. Now William was thinking about his father, and George, with customary common sense, had moved on to a topic he *could* influence. 'How about shopping? I need a new sports bag.'

'Another one? I don't think so,' Poppy said drily. 'We could go swimming.'

'Nah—we did that on Tuesday. How about the dry ski slope? I want to try snow-boarding.'

Poppy's heart sank. 'I don't think your father would like that.'

'He wouldn't know—'

'Who wouldn't know what?'

George jumped guiltily at the sound of his father's voice. 'Nothing,' he mumbled.

'George was suggesting a trip to a dry ski slope tomorrow to do snow-boarding,' Poppy explained, earning herself a black look from George.

'Actually,' James said, flipping a chair round and straddling it, 'I was thinking of taking tomorrow off and taking you boys to the zoo.'

Their eyes widened, then they whooped with delight and flung themselves at him. 'Can we buy food for the llamas?' William wanted to know.

'I don't know. I expect so.'

'Will there be elephants?'

'Possibly. It depends which zoo we go to.'

'Will Poppy come?'

James met her eyes then. 'I hope so. The zoo was her idea originally. If she abandons me now I'll be sunk.'

Poppy pretended to consider it for the benefit of the boys, but there was no question of it. A day out with James and his sons? She wouldn't miss it for the world. She finally nodded her consent. 'All right, then. I'll come—but I think you'll need an early night. Tired boys don't get zoo trips, because they whinge.'

The boys disappeared like snow in the Sahara. Half an hour later they were tucked up in bed, she had read them a story and was back down in the kitchen.

James was peering hopefully in the fridge. 'Anything to eat?' he asked her.

'Steak,' she told him, 'with jacket potato and salad. OK?'

He nodded. 'Lovely. What about you?'

'I ate with the boys. We weren't sure what time you'd be coming back.' She set the frying pan on the heat and turned to him. 'About this trip tomorrow—have you really got time?'

He laughed. 'Not really, but I'll make time. Why?'

'Because you can't go messing them about. You've said you'll take them—'

'And I will. Poppy, I know I've let them down in the past, but I really will be here tomorrow.'

She would believe it when she saw it, she decided. Only an idiot believed everything they were told. She cooked his meal, watched his back as he disappeared into the library, bearing the plate in one hand and a glass of wine in the other, and started clearing up the mess, throwing the plates into the dishwasher with scant regard for their safety.

'"Thank you, that looks delicious",' she parroted. '"You're an angel, Poppy—"'

'Poppy?'

She spun round, her hand on her heart, hot colour flooding her cheeks. 'Did you have to sneak up on me?'

His grin was crooked and hesitant. 'Sorry. I came to get some mustard.' The grin faded under her glower. 'Look, have I done something wrong?' he asked.

'You?' She stared at him in amazement. 'I thought it was me that had done something wrong! You've hardly spoken to me since we left my parents' on Sunday.'

He groaned, turning half away, then turned back. His eyes, she noticed absently, were tired. Tired and a little bleak. 'I promised your mother I'd take care of you, that you were safe with me.'

'Does that mean we can't speak?' Poppy asked, puzzled.

He sighed. 'No, of course not. It just means that I have difficulty trusting myself around you. You're a lovely girl, Poppy. I'd have to be dead from the neck down not to notice you.'

She blushed, warm colour sweeping her cheek in a faint tide and stealing her breath away. 'Is that all?' she asked, relief making her giddy.

'All?' James said in disbelief. '*All?* I can't look at you without embarrassing myself,' he told her candidly.

She grinned. 'You're no slouch yourself,' she said softly.

He swore, quietly but succinctly, and met her eyes, his own heated. 'OK, we're both aware of it, but nothing's going to happen, Poppy. I want you to know that. I can't give you white lace and promises.'

Poppy laughed gently, dredging up a careless smile. 'James, have I asked you to? So you're a reasonably presentable man with the advantage of scads of dosh. You also have more hang-ups than the average washing line. I'd be crazy to get involved with you. I could end up spending the rest of my life separating you and the boys every time you had a fight!' She smiled at him to soften her words. 'Thanks, but no, thanks. I think I'll stick to my bucolic farmer.'

She hoped she fooled James. She certainly didn't fool herself. The image of her bucolic farmer was miles away, lost in the mists of time, firmly supplanted by the tall, powerful man who was cluttering up her kitchen. His kitchen. Whatever.

She shoved her hands in her pockets so she didn't grab him, and leant back against the edge of the sink. 'Your steak will be cold.'

He blinked, then seemed to collect himself. His mouth firmed as if he was clamping in a retort, and he found the mustard in the cupboard and left her alone.

The breath whooshed out of her lungs in a little flurry, and she rammed her hands into her hair and rolled her eyes. She was right, she would be crazy to get involved with him, but that wouldn't stop it happening. 'Oh, damn,' she muttered, and turned her attentions back to the dishwasher.

'Dad, look! We can buy food!'

'So we can.' James rummaged in his pocket for change, and bought two bags of special food for the animals, handing one each to the boys.

'Don't I get one?' Poppy teased.

George and William turned instantly. 'Buy her one, Dad!'

She smiled and shook her head. 'I'll share yours.'
They ran ahead, darting here and there, clearly having a
wonderful time. James and Poppy followed behind, their
efforts to impose a system thwarted by the boys' curious
minds and faster legs. They seemed to come back again
and again to the penguins, however, particularly the
fuzzy little South African baby penguins, by whom the
boys seemed inordinately enthralled.

Then suddenly, when Poppy's legs were aching and
her feet were freezing and her nose was bright pink with
cold, the boys lost interest in the zoo altogether.

'Can we go home now?' they said.

They had been missing for a few minutes, and had
been found, fairly predictably, near the penguins. However, now they had had enough, and George said he
didn't feel very well.

They did, indeed, both have a rather hectic colour in
their cheeks, Poppy thought, and George was hunched
over as if he had stomach ache, and so they were bun-
dled back into the car and taken home. They were quiet
in the car, but Poppy thought she felt an undercurrent of
excitement that years of instinct told her not to trust.
When they arrived back at the house the boys poured
out of the car and rushed in, suddenly recovered.

'I feel better now—I think I'll have a bath,' George
said.

And William, mumbling, 'Me too,' ran off up the
stairs after him.

'What about your coats?' Poppy called, but they were
gone. 'How odd,' she muttered, and went back into the
kitchen. James was hanging up his jacket on the hook
by the door.

'How are they?' he asked.

'Fine. I don't understand. I don't trust it.'

James shrugged. 'They're just kids. Who knows how their minds work? I gave up trying to understand them years ago. How about a cup of tea? My feet are killing me and I think I'm on the verge of pneumonia. I would have been better off at work.'

'You loved it, confess,' Poppy teased, and James laughed drily.

'So I did. Thank you for reminding me.'

'My pleasure.' Poppy put the kettle on, made a pot of tea and passed a cup to James. Overhead they could hear bathwater running, and the occasional giggle.

'They sound all right,' James said, stretching his long legs out under the table with a sigh.

There was a shriek and a splash, and Poppy shut her eyes. 'Just remember I have to clear up that mess they're making,' she reminded him. 'Perhaps I'll go and read the riot act.'

'Have your tea first,' James coaxed. 'It can't get any worse.'

She was tempted. Terribly tempted. He looked wonderful, relaxed and comfortable and good enough to eat. She could have sat opposite him and studied him all day, the crisp brown curls clustered round that strong, well-shaped head, the straight bar of his brows above those astonishingly beautiful gold-green eyes, the slightly crooked plane of his nose slashing his face in half, leading her eyes down to his mouth, the firm, full lips that felt so good against hers, the stubble-roughened skin stretched taut over the strong line of his jaw, its texture so tempting to her hand—

There was a crash and a scream from above, and Poppy all but dropped her tea and sprinted for the stairs, hotly pursued by James.

They burst into the bathroom and stopped in their tracks.

The boys squirmed guiltily. They were sitting on the bathroom floor, still fully dressed, and in the bath, swimming happily in a foot or so of water, was a baby South African penguin.

'Oh, my God,' James said with feeling. He leant back against the doorframe and studied the little bird with horror. 'What the hell is that?'

'A baby penguin,' George offered nervously.

'I can see that,' James said with deadly calm. 'Right. Boys, out of here, please. Get yourselves cleaned up and changed and wait for me in the sitting room. Poppy, guard that—' he gestured at the little ball of fluff swimming cheerfully in the bath '—with your life.'

'What are you going to do?' Poppy asked as the boys scampered off down the corridor.

'Do? I'm going to ring the zoo, then I'm going to get the boys and wring their necks.'

He left the room, and Poppy perched on the edge of the loo and watched the little bird. It seemed quite happy. She checked the water, relieved to find it was cold, and wondered if she should give it something to eat. What, though? A tin of sardines?

Better wait for the zoo's response.

It wasn't long coming. James reappeared in the doorway looking less than thrilled, the cordless phone in his hand, and studied the hapless penguin.

'It looks all right,' he said into the phone. His face was flushed with embarrassment, and he nodded. 'Yes, I quite appreciate that. Of course, I'll pay any necessary recovery costs and veterinary bills. Yes, of course. We'll keep an eye on it—no, we won't let it out; it's in the bathroom and the window's shut. It's in the bath—cold water? I don't know.'

Poppy nodded frantically, and James relayed the information, apologised yet again and finally hung up.

'Ouch,' he said, rubbing his ear. 'They weren't pleased. Apparently baby penguins are very susceptible to aspergillosis, especially under stress.'

'Poor little chap.'

She reached out to the penguin and it pecked her. So much for her gesture of friendship. 'What about food?' she asked, rubbing her hand.

He shook his head. 'We do nothing. They're on the way. I could kill those boys.' He said it mildly, but Poppy wasn't fooled. He was furious, and this time, she realised, they had gone too far.

The penguin's life could be at risk, and it was their fault. She sighed inwardly. Why had she suggested a zoo trip? she wondered.

'Why don't you let the zoo man who comes for it have a word with them?' she suggested.

James laughed without humour. 'Good idea. He certainly cut me down to size at a stroke. Perhaps he'd like to take charge of their upbringing—maybe they've got a spare cage? On second thoughts he's probably got more sense—they're too much of a liability!'

Poppy smiled at him, hoping to defuse his anger, but he just sighed in frustration and slid down the bathroom wall until he was sitting on the floor, legs bent up, arms resting on his knees, his back propped against the tiles.

'Why my kids, Poppy?'

She smiled again to comfort him. 'Perhaps they need a pet?'

'Pet? A pet? Are you crazy?'

'James, most kids have pets. Didn't you have one as a child?'

He shrugged. 'There was an old cat. I had a hamster, too, for a while. The cat ate it.'

Poppy stifled a giggle, and James glared at her. 'Poppy, it really isn't funny. That man from the zoo was furious.'

'I'm sure he was. Don't worry, James, the penguin's all right.'

'You can't tell. Apparently it takes up to three weeks to be sure it won't succumb to the aspergillosis after the stress.'

'Oh.'

'Yes, "oh". Poor little blighter.'

'I thought there was something up in the car.'

James snorted. 'We should have smelled a rat when they wanted to leave so suddenly. Well, I can tell you, I won't leave anywhere with them again without frisking them both thoroughly! Are we sure they haven't got a tarantula or a snake here as well?'

Poppy chuckled. 'I think we're safe on that front. The penguin was more than enough for them. I tell you what, why don't you guard this little chap and I'll go and check with the boys and get supper on while we wait for the zoo—OK?'

She found the boys in the sitting room, wide-eyed and very subdued. 'That was a bit daft, wasn't it?' she said calmly. William began to cry.

'Dad'll kill us,' he sniffed.

'I doubt it,' Poppy said drily. 'He might want to, but I have to say I think this time you deserve it.'

'Poppy, talk to him,' they pleaded.

She shook her head. 'No. You're his children, he has a right to discipline you. You've been very foolish and irresponsible, and you'll have to suffer the consequences. So, unfortunately, will the penguin. Apparently it might become ill and possibly even die. You might like to think about that while you wait for the man from the zoo.'

She reached the door, then turned back. 'You didn't by any chance bring anything else home with you?'

They shook their heads.

'I'm so pleased.' She went into the kitchen, wondering if she'd been too hard on them, and then decided no, she hadn't. They had to learn that James could be fair and reasonable even when he was furious, as he now was. She just hoped he would justify her faith in him and not take them apart limb by limb!

The man from the zoo was very straight with the boys. Apart from the trouble he had been put to, he explained, there was the question of theft, endangering wildlife, causing unnecessary suffering, traumatising a young animal and exposing it to the possible risk of a fatal stress-induced disease.

By the time he had finished the boys were both in tears and vowed never to do anything so foolish again.

'I should ban you both from the zoo for life,' he went on, 'but I've got a better idea. Rather than take this to the police, I think I'll ask your father to make a donation to the zoo—perhaps the lifetime adoption of this penguin, for instance.'

Poppy saw James's jaw clench. 'How much is that?' he asked tightly.

'Fifty pounds a year for life.'

'And how long do they live?'

The man smiled, clearly enjoying James's discomfiture. 'About thirty years.'

'Thir—that's fifteen hundred pounds!' Poppy exclaimed in a shocked whisper. The boys' eyes widened, but James said nothing, just took out his chequebook and wrote out a cheque for two thousand in grim-lipped silence.

'Here,' he said, handing over the cheque. 'I'm sorry we've been such a nuisance. I hope the penguin doesn't suffer any repercussions.'

'So do I. Thank you for your donation.'

James snorted. 'My pleasure.'

The boys shadowed him to the door, then as he was leaving George said, 'Can we come and see him again, if we promise to be good?'

The zoo keeper looked down at them and relented a little. 'If your parents keep you under very strict control.'

'They'll be handcuffed to my side—if I'm ever fool enough to bring them back,' James assured him.

He nodded, then, picking up the cage with the penguin safely inside it, he left. James turned to the boys. 'Bed, I think.'

'But we haven't had supper!'

William tugged George's arm. 'Come on. I don't think we get supper.'

Poppy looked at James, and he shook his head. Oh, dear, she thought. Still, they had been very naughty. One night without supper might just serve to make them think about their actions in future.

'Clean your teeth and get ready for bed, and I'll come up and see you in a few minutes,' she told them. She watched them trail across the hall and up the stairs, then turned to James.

'I'm sorry.'

He looked at her in amazement. 'Sorry? What for?'

She shrugged. 'It was my idea.'

He chuckled humourlessly. 'Poppy, they're my children. I have to take the ultimate responsibility. The government says they have to go to school. If they're naughty at school, does that make it the Education Minister's fault?'

She laughed. 'Probably not. Come on, our supper's ready and I'm starving.'

James followed her into the kitchen. 'I expect the boys are, too. Do you think sending them to bed without any supper is too harsh?'

'Harsh?' Poppy grinned at him. 'I think not. I imagine they'll think they got away with it lightly. Come on. Let them stew for a while. You can take them a sandwich later if you feel too guilty.'

He snorted. 'Guilty? Why should I feel guilty? *They* stole the penguin!' He pulled out a chair and dropped into it, propping his elbow on the table and resting his chin on his fist. 'That has to be the most expensive zoo trip on record.'

'Hmm.' Poppy dished up the chicken casserole and set the plate down in front of him. 'I take it the money's not the real issue?'

He arched a brow. 'You mean, can I afford it? I should think so.'

'Then tell yourself you've done some good, and relax.'

She set her plate down, plonked two glasses on the table between them and sloshed some wine into them. 'Cheers.'

He smiled over the rim and shook his head. 'Cheers.'

Then he put down the glass, picked up his knife and fork and set about demolishing his meal. As she ate, Poppy watched him clean his plate with evident enjoyment.

'It hasn't spoilt you, has it?'

He looked up. 'Pardon?'

'The money. It hasn't spoilt you—being rich. I mean, here you are, eating a simple stew in the kitchen with the hired help, when you could be running a fleet of servants and living in the lap of luxury.'

He laughed self-consciously. 'That's not me, though. Anyway, I don't think of you as the hired help, Poppy. Perhaps it would be better if I did.'

'Helen does,' she said before she could stop herself.

His laugh was bitter. 'Yes, no doubt. Helen's very into hired help. She thinks I should have a butler and a man-servant and a chauffeur, of all things. I keep telling her it isn't necessary, but I think she feels I let myself down—don't project the right image, you know? Mr Successful should have all the trappings of wealth.' He shrugged. 'It's not me, Poppy. I like my home to be a home. That's why I hate that bloody awful drawing room. When are you going to deal with it?'

She eyed him steadily. 'Do you really mean it?'

'Sure. How much do you want?'

'I don't know. The furniture and carpets will be the killer.'

'Ten thousand? Fifteen?'

Poppy laughed. 'Do people often rip you off?'

His smile was wry. 'They try. Why?'

'I was thinking more like a tenth of that. The curtains just need the pelmets relining with something colourful, and perhaps an echo of that on the edge, and the cushions will be very cheap because I'll make them. The carpet you'll have to choose with me—'

'Why? I trust you.'

She blinked. 'You do? We *could* be talking thousands for that.'

He shrugged. 'Poppy, you won't cheat me; I know that. I'll get a local firm to come round with some fabric samples, and I'll contact a local auction house and arrange an account for you so you can start going to sales and having fun. If it's a fine art house they might have some old rugs that would do the job. OK?'

It was more than OK, it sounded wonderful. It sounded, in fact, like playing house, and it hit Poppy like a ton of bricks. While James made the boys a sandwich and went upstairs to them with it to make his peace, Poppy sat in the kitchen nursing another glass of wine and wondering what on earth she was getting herself into.

Cosy suppers, an unlimited budget to redo the drawing room and turn it into a home—was she going to survive? OK, he'd promised nothing would happen. That wouldn't stop her falling for him, though, not by a country mile. Just as being on a diet didn't stop you wanting chocolates, so making rash promises wouldn't stop either of them from succumbing to the attraction.

She sighed and dropped her head onto her arms. Damn James Carmichael for being so attractive and charming and downright normal. And damn her stupid hormones for wanting him.

She didn't hear him come back in, but she knew he was there. All her senses stood on end, and she felt her heart pick up. His hands rested lightly on her shoulders, kneading gently at the taut muscles.

'You're tired,' he murmured. 'You should go to bed.'

She sat up, leaning back against the chair with her head dropped forwards. 'Don't stop,' she mumbled. 'That's wonderful.'

His hands worked into the muscles round her shoulders and neck, the fingers strong and yet gentle, easing out the kinks. She rolled her head back and found his hard, flat abdomen right behind her, radiating warmth. His hands slid up and cupped her cheeks, tilting her head backwards, and then he bent over and laid a kiss against her lips.

She moaned and turned on the chair, and he drew her up into his arms, his mouth gentle at first, tentative. Then his control snapped and his mouth became greedy and demanding, his tongue searching hers out, plundering her secrets, laying waste to her self-control.

She moaned and arched against him, and felt a deep shudder run through him. He was aroused, hard and hot and hungry, and she wanted to scream with frustration because the boys were in the house and still awake, and they weren't supposed to be doing this, anyway, and any second now he'd remember—

'Damn,' he groaned against her mouth, and, lifting his head, he tucked her under his chin and rocked her hard against his chest. 'Damn, damn, damn, damn, damn.'

'You shouldn't make rash promises,' she teased with the last shreds of her sense of humour.

He gave a hollow laugh. 'No, but I did, and I meant it. I'm sure if you give me time I'll remember why.' He eased away from her and stood at the window, staring out over the dark garden. 'I want you, Poppy,' he said quietly. 'I'm not sure this promise is going to be one I can keep.'

'So why bother?' she asked after a moment.

'Why?' He turned, and his eyes still blazed with need. 'Because I'm not good for you. Because I won't use you like that. Because you deserve better.'

'You do yourself an injustice,' she told him softly. 'I'm an adult, James. Perhaps you should let me make up my own mind about us.'

'There is no "us". That's the point. My life's enough of a mess, Poppy, without mixing business with pleasure. I need you for the boys, as I told your mother. I can't afford to let my needs—or yours—get in the way of that.'

'Are they mutually exclusive?' she asked.

He shrugged. 'I don't know. All I know is that the boys have suffered enough hardship and trauma in their short lives. You're good for them. I can't jeopardise that for the sake of a temporary diversion, and I can't let you do it, either. I'm sorry, Poppy—you'll never know how much.' Then he turned on his heel and went out of the kitchen, leaving her alone with her tumbling emotions.

CHAPTER SIX

A FEW days later, and, she imagined, as part of his policy of keeping his distance, James told Poppy she ought to have some time off. A formal arrangement was long overdue, but it didn't stop Poppy feeling rejected when James announced that she would have Sunday and Monday off in future.

'If I'm not going out or entertaining on the Saturday night, you can go home then, of course, and I'll get the children to school on Monday mornings and arrange for their collection on Monday afternoons. I've found a woman through the headmaster who'll be willing to have them after school, for a small consideration,' he told Poppy, in a dry tone that gave her an idea of how 'small' the consideration wasn't, 'and so you needn't return till late on Monday, ready for Tuesday morning.'

And that was that. She now had weekends, after a fashion.

She should have been delighted.

The first weekend was the one after the boys had returned to school for the second half of the spring term, and on Saturday evening Poppy duly set off for home. She expected to have a wonderful and long-overdue rest.

Instead she missed them all. Her family, boisterous and open-hearted though they were, still couldn't fill the gap left by James and his children, and she mooched around and got underfoot until Monday morning. Then she came down to the kitchen to find her mother nursing a new-born orphaned lamb.

'What happened?' she asked, automatically putting the kettle on the Aga and wrapping a pinny round her waist to take the lamb. The lambs were always her job.

'First twin died. Your father pulled this one out in the nick of time, but we lost the mother.'

'Can we find a foster-mother?'

Audrey Taylor smiled benignly. 'Possibly. I thought, though, for now, it might be nice to have him in the kitchen and spoil him a bit. I wondered if the boys might like to see him, and help feed him, maybe?'

Poppy's foolish heart jumped at the idea, but she quelled it. 'I'm sure they'd love it, but they're going to someone else after school, it's all arranged.'

'I'm sure it could be unarranged,' Audrey suggested gently. 'You could bring them back here for supper— they'd love it so much, Poppy, and they don't get to see many animals.'

Poppy was a push-over. She knew it, her mother knew it, anybody who had met her for thirty seconds knew it. 'OK,' she found herself agreeing. 'But I'll have to clear it with James first.'

She rang the house, hoping to catch him before he left with the boys, but he had already gone and all she got was the answering machine. She tried the office later, but he was in a meeting, and she didn't dare pull another stunt like the last one, when she'd told the secretary the twins were in hospital!

She'd have to go to the office in person, she decided. She knew vaguely where it was, although she'd never been there. She'd leave in time to go to his office and then fetch the boys from school, assuming he said yes. Of course, he might not.

She kissed her mother goodbye, promising to be back later, and set off for Norwich in James's 'little'

Mercedes. She was getting all too used to pottering around in such style, she thought to herself in disgust. So much for the ancient bangers and her mother's modest little car that she had been used to up to now.

She sighed. Luxury was becoming altogether too familiar, she thought wryly. She was in danger of getting spoiled.

She found the office complex without difficulty. The only thing she had difficulty with was making her mouth work at the gate to the car park, because the whole set-up was enormous and screamed success, and it came home to Poppy with a bump that her boss was actually a very powerful and significant individual.

'Can I see your ID?' the gatekeeper asked.

She shut her mouth with a snap and swallowed. 'Um—I've come to see Mr Carmichael—I'm his nanny. Poppy Taylor. Hang on, I've got my driving licence— oh, and this is his car.'

He peered at her driving licence, then the car. 'Hold on a moment, please,' he said, and went back inside his little hut and consulted a list, then emerged with a smile.

'That's all right, Miss Taylor, you've got clearance. Would you mind pinning this badge on, please?'

And that was it. She was through his evidently tight security, and, following the arrows and road signs, she made her way to the visitors' car park by the entrance to the office.

She went into Reception, wearing her visitor's badge, and asked the dark-haired girl at the desk for James.

'Do you have an appointment?'

'No—I'm his nanny. I just need to ask him something about the boys.'

The girl smiled. 'You're very brave. I gather they're

terrors. Take the lift and go up to the third floor and turn right. Mr Carmichael's office is at the end.'

Poppy went as directed, considering who might have given the girl the idea that the boys were terrors. Helen? Probably.

She found her way blocked by another minion, this one a redhead and just as well groomed. Poppy was extremely conscious of her jeans and boots by now, but she reminded herself that the redhead wasn't about to pick up twin hooligans and go and feed lambs in a farm kitchen. She'd look pretty ridiculous in her black mini-skirt and four-inch heels.

'He's in a meeting,' Poppy was told.

'He's always in a meeting. Could you ask him to pop out so I could have a word, please?'

She shook her head. 'I'm sorry, I can't interrupt.'

'Please?' Poppy said patiently. 'It is important.'

'What's it about? I'll slip in and have a word with him.'

Poppy nearly laughed. This was going to sound great! 'I want to take the boys back to my parents' farm this evening to feed a lamb.'

The girl's eyes widened. 'A lamb? You want me to interrupt an important meeting to ask Mr Carmichael if you can feed a lamb?'

Poppy nodded. 'Yes, please.'

The girl's eyes shot to a closed mahogany door, then back to Poppy. 'I can't do that—'

'Then I will,' Poppy said calmly, and crossing the hall she opened the door and went in, ignoring the little shriek of protest from the redhead behind her.

James was in full flood, but at the sight of Poppy he excused himself and hurried over to her, arriving at Poppy's side at the same time as the redhead.

'Mr Carmichael, I'm sorry. She just—'

'Poppy, what the hell—?'

'James, I'm sorry, I needed to see you and your guard-dog wouldn't interrupt you.'

He shot the girl a reassuring smile, cut off her apology and sent her back to her desk, then turned to Poppy.

'What have they done now?'

Poppy laughed softly. 'Nothing. Relax. We had a lamb born in the night and he's lost his mother. Mum wondered if the boys would like to feed him, so I thought if you didn't mind I could get them from school and take them over, and then we could have supper there and come back later.'

James thrust a hand through his much-tousled hair and shot her a grin. 'Feeding orphaned lambs—sounds a bit bucolic.'

'Absolutely.'

Something wistful and filled with longing flittered through his eyes. 'Can I come?' he asked softly.

Poppy's mouth fell open. 'Wha—yes, of course, but you're busy. These people—'

His mouth tipped wryly. 'They'll keep. We've virtually finished, anyway.' He turned back to his companions, who were watching them openly and with fascination. 'Sorry, ladies and gentlemen, something's come up. I'm going to have to leave you. Helen, could I hand the chair over to you, please, to wind up the meeting and sort out the final details? I have two small boys and an orphaned lamb that require my attention.'

Helen's jaw dropped a little, but she recovered herself with commendable skill.

'Of course. Your children must come first.'

Poppy's eyebrows shot up, but James just grinned.

'Glad we agree. I'm sure you'll find Helen is able to answer all your questions, everyone. Please excuse us.'

There was a gracious and accepting murmur, and Poppy hid a smile as he swept her out of the door, to the total amazement of the redhead, who was sitting stunned at her desk, still waiting for the axe to fall.

'Hold the fort, Sue,' he said with a wink at the astonished girl. 'I'm going to feed a lamb—I'll be in tomorrow.'

Poppy nearly choked on a laugh. 'I think she thought you were going to sack her,' she told James in the lift.

'Sue? Nah. I'll give her a rise and tell her to use her initiative. It works wonders.'

Poppy chuckled. 'Did you see her face? She can't believe you're doing this.'

His mouth tipped. 'Shall I tell you something, Poppy? Neither can I, but it feels great.'

His laugh, warm and mellow, rang softly in the lift and made Poppy's heart feel lighter. Wow, he was making some progress!

The lamb was a real hit with the boys. Audrey had to prise it away from them when its little tummy was positively bursting, just to stop them killing it with kindness.

'He needs to sleep,' she said gently but firmly, and settled the little chap under a heat lamp in the corner of the small barn they used for the lambing, near some other new lambs with their mothers. He bleated pitifully, and Poppy saw the boys waver.

'Can't he be inside?' they asked hopefully.

Poppy chuckled. 'No. He's got to learn to cope with the cold. He'll be all right.'

As they crossed the farmyard Audrey pulled her coat tighter round her neck and shivered. 'Oh, that wind goes right through me. There's more snow forecast for later in the week.'

'Again?' Poppy said, amazed. 'I thought we'd finished with the snow.'

'Apparently not. Oooh, it's bitter. Come on, boys, in by the stove and let's get supper on, shall we?'

'Can we feed the lamb again later?' William asked.

'Much later,' Audrey agreed. 'Let's feed you all first. Poppy, call your brothers, darling. They're in the stock barn.'

They all came in, sitting down round the big old table in the kitchen and tucking into Audrey's rich, sustaining stew. Poppy watched James eating the simple but nourishing meal with relish, and thought of the empire-builder that he was and the impressive headquarters of his enormous operation she had seen today.

The Taylors' homely kitchen was a far cry from the deep-pile carpets and designer prints of his boardroom, and yet he seemed quite at ease in either.

So at ease, in fact, that he seemed happy to stay for a second and even a third cup of coffee after supper. They stayed in the kitchen, all clustered round the table playing cards and cheating furiously, until finally at nine Poppy's father stood up and went out to do the final stock check. Twenty minutes later he was back, stamping snow off his boots, banging the door shut quickly behind him.

'I don't think you people are going anywhere tonight,' he said gravely. 'Damned snow's at it again—there's a regular blizzard out there.'

'What?' James came to his feet and crossed to the door, opening it a crack and staring blankly out across the yard. A moment later he shut the door and turned to Poppy, his eyes wide with astonishment. 'I can't even see the barn. It's just a whiteout. It's come out of no-where.'

'You'd better stay the night—Poppy, the boys can go together in the spare room,' Audrey said, 'and James can have the room next to you. The bed isn't enormous, but it's comfortable and it beats being stuck in a blizzard.'

'I wouldn't dream of putting you to so much trouble —' James began, but Audrey cut him off with a wave of her hand.

'And I wouldn't dream of letting you take the boys out in this weather except in extreme emergency. Poppy, love, give me a hand with the sheets, could you?'

James put a hand on Audrey's shoulder and pushed her gently back into her chair. 'Poppy and I can do it—you sit here.'

She looked at him in amazement. 'Are you sure?'

His mouth tipped. 'I do know how to make a bed.'

'Of course you do, but you've been busy all day—'

'And you haven't?'

She smiled. 'Go on, then. You and Poppy go and do it. You know where the sheets are, darling?'

Poppy nodded and led the way upstairs. How was James going to take this? she wondered. She had caught a glimpse of the snow, flying horizontally, and knew that the farm would be cut off by morning. The fine white powder would blow off the field opposite and fill up the lane, and that would be it—till Tom went out with the tractor and cleared it.

Poppy wondered how hard she'd have to bribe Tom not to clear the lane until later, to give James and the boys a day together in the snow...

She reached the top of the stairs and pulled fresh sheets out of the airing cupboard, then led James into the boys' room.

They made up the twin beds quickly, then went into the little room next to Poppy's. There was a communicating door, and James eyed it thoughtfully.

'Will I be safe?' he murmured with a slight smile.

Poppy met his eyes, and her heart jerked in her chest. 'Safe?' she said with a little grin. 'I would think so— unless you count the spiders.'

He chuckled, but as they bent over the bed and their hands touched Poppy felt heat shoot up her arm and almost jerked away. Lord, she only had to be in the same room as him and her hormones went crazy! What was wrong with her?

They went back down and found the family had moved through to the drawing room. Tom and the boys were sprawled in front of the fire with Bridie, and she was lying on her back, tongue lolling, lapping up the boys' attention.

'Shameless hussy,' Tom growled affectionately, and her tail swooshed happily. Poppy checked her watch, and gave the boys a meaningful look.

'Oh, Poppy, not yet!' George pleaded, hugging the dog against his chest. 'We have to feed the lamb!'

'Yeah—poor Hector. He'll be hungry and cold—'

Poppy's laugh cut them off. 'That little chap won't be hungry for hours, and there's no way he can be cold under the heat lamp. Come on.'

They went, and after she had tucked them in she went back down and settled herself in the corner of the sofa with her tapestry, watching James and her father out of the corner of her eye. Her brothers went up to bed, then her parents, leaving her alone with James and the dog and instructions to feed the lamb one last time and take the dog out before they retired for the night.

'Will we disturb them if we don't go up now?' James asked her.

She shook her head. 'Not if we're quiet. Why?'

He met her eyes. 'Because I just want to sit here with you for a while by the fire, and…'

'And?'

He shrugged. 'Just sit.'

Poppy smiled. 'How bucolic.'

His chuckle was rich and warm. He got up, leaving his armchair and coming to sit at the other end of the settee. Poppy had her feet up, and he tucked them into his lap and rubbed her cold toes. 'You're freezing,' he told her.

'My toes are always like ice.'

'You should wear shoes.'

'I hate shoes.'

He shook his head and bent over, huffing hot air into her socks and making her toes curl. The look in his eyes was every bit as hot, and she felt her heart trip and race a little, sticking in her throat and jamming the breath so she had to think how to drag the air in and out.

'James…' she began, but her words trailed to a halt and he lungs suddenly started working overtime. He lifted his head, his eyes riveted by the rapid rise and fall of her breasts under the ancient sweatshirt, and then he looked up and met her eyes, and the raw need in his was nearly her undoing.

She swung her feet to the ground and stood up, dropping her tapestry back in the bag and wondering how much she would have to unpick to get rid of her mistakes. 'We ought to feed Hector,' she said, and her voice sounded scrapy and out of practice.

She didn't wait to see if he would follow, but clicked her fingers for Bridie and went out into the kitchen. He was right behind her. 'Here,' she said, chucking him her father's old thick parka and boots, 'put these on if you're coming out.' Then, tugging on her coat and boots, she headed for the door.

'Where do you get the milk?' he asked, appearing at her shoulder as she turned the handle and stepped out into the howling blizzard.

'I have to milk one of the old ewes,' she yelled over the noise.

The screaming wind drove the snow straight into their faces, and she tucked her head down and ran across the yard, Bridie bouncing at her side and James behind her. They all but fell into the barn, and Poppy banged the snow off her shoulders and shook her hair to free it of the tiny dry flakes.

James fingered the snow on his jacket. 'It's very dry,' he murmured. 'It'll settle.'

Poppy nodded. 'We'll be cut off by the morning with this wind.' She met his eyes. 'Will that be an insurmountable problem?'

He shrugged. 'It won't have to be. Do you have a fax modem?'

She chuckled. 'We're poor farmers, James. What do you think?'

He smiled, and she felt guilty for deliberately misleading him, even if it was for his own sake. The fact was they had an office filled with computer equipment of one sort or another, and they had been on the Internet for years. The trouble was, if he knew that, he'd spend the day communicating with his office and not having fun with the boys—and with her.

She stifled her guilt. He deserved a day playing truant. It would do him good. Let the Frisbee earn her keep holding the fort. Doubtless the bossy creature would be in her element.

'Helen will cope,' she said encouragingly. 'Here, hold this.' She handed him a little pail, scraped her hair back into a ponytail band and took the pail from him again, then, kneeling down in one of the pens, she milked one of the old, patient ewes with the competence born of years of practice. She poured the milk into Hector's bottle and screwed on the teat, went over to the lamb's pen and climbed in with him. 'Join me?' she offered, scooting over on the straw to make room for James beside her.

He hesitated for a second or two, then, hitching up his trousers, he clambered over the side of the pen, eyed the straw suspiciously and lowered himself down beside her.

There was only barely enough room, so the hard length of his thigh was trapped against hers, and the jut of his hip pressed her side, and because there was nowhere else for his arm to go he put it round her. He was tense for a moment, then with a muted sigh he settled his hand against her shoulder and squeezed gently. Poppy felt a surge of affection—and something else. Something much more troubling that she didn't want to confront, at least not yet. She put it aside and concentrated on the lamb.

He was hungry, butting the bottle and clamouring for his food, and she tipped the bottle, put the teat in Hector's greedy little mouth and smiled. 'Better now?' she asked him softly.

'Looks better to me,' James said quietly from just behind her.

With a contented sigh she leant against him, rested her head against his shoulder and closed her eyes. Hector was butting and slurping at the bottle, there were warm

shufflings and grunts from the other pens, and Poppy
thought it wouldn't be a bad sort of place to be born.
Everyone felt sorry for Mary and Joseph, but it could
have been worse. The animals gave the whole thing a
sort of earthy peace—unlike the clinical efficiency of a
modern teaching hospital. She'd done part of her nursery
nurse training in a hospital delivery unit, and she'd hated
it. After home it had seemed so noisy and technical.

This—this was bliss by comparison. Apart from anything else, she had James to lean on.

Hector finished his bottle and snuggled down against
her leg, and she tilted her head and looked at James.

'OK?' she asked softly.

He nodded. 'Has he finished?'

'Yes.'

'Good.' Then his hand came up and captured her chin,
and his mouth settled softly over hers.

Heat exploded in her, and with a muffled cry she
moved into his arms and lost herself in the magic of his
kiss. She slid her hands up round his neck and buried
her fingers in his hair, sampling the soft, silky curls,
testing the texture, tousling them curiously. She wondered if his chest had hair on it and, if so, how it would
feel, but there were too many clothes in the way and
besides, it would be crazy to take this kiss any further.

As if he read her mind, James lifted his head and
dropped a gentle kiss on her brow. 'We ought to go back
inside,' he murmured huskily.

'Mmm.' Still she lingered, her fingers threaded
through that wonderfully silky hair, and then at last she
moved away. Her fingers felt cold, a little bereft. With
a sigh she eased the sleeping lamb under the lamp, built
up the straw round him to make a little nest and then

stood, brushing the loose straw from the back of her coat.

James followed her out of the pen, then, whistling up Bridie, she checked the two collies in their kennel, topped up their water and ran back across the farmyard, her head tucked down to dodge the whirling snow.

They all but fell into the kitchen, laughing at their headlong flight from the elements. They kicked off their boots, hung up their coats and then Poppy went over to the Aga, leant against the front and grinned at James. 'Fun, eh? Not exactly what you thought you'd be doing when you left for work this morning!'

'Not exactly,' he said, returning her grin, 'but you're right, it is fun. Especially some of it.'

Heat brushed her cheeks, as she remembered the kiss in the warmth of Hector's pen, and she turned and picked up the kettle.

'Fancy a cup of tea or coffee before we turn in?' she offered a little breathlessly.

'Cocoa?' he said hopefully.

'Sure.' She put milk on to heat, heaped cocoa into the mugs with loads of sugar, then poured the boiling milk on and stirred it before dolloping cream on the top.

'Cream?' He sounded scandalised.

Poppy grinned. 'Have to do it properly.'

She dropped into a chair, stuck her feet up on another one and sighed with contentment. She would definitely have to bribe Tom not to get the tractor out too early tomorrow, she thought. Sitting here like this with James was just altogether too addictive.

'Tell me about the farm,' James said lazily, sprawling out with his cocoa in one hand and fondling the dog's ears with the other. So Poppy told him how many acres they had of what crops, and what livestock they kept now, and how it had changed since she'd been a child, and although she couldn't believe he wasn't bored to death he didn't seem to be.

Finally, though, she couldn't suppress her yawns any longer. She was tired, and although she wanted nothing more than to stay here with James all night, she knew it was foolish to sit up so long. The twins would be up at the crack of dawn regardless of how much or how little sleep Poppy had managed to fit in. Anyway, her parents would be half awake until they heard the house settle for the night, so it was only fair to go up.

She led James up the back way to the little landing outside their rooms, and then tipped her head back to look up at him. She considered giving him a kiss, but then thought better of it. She might not be able to trust herself to stop at a kiss, and her parents were just down the landing and doubtless listening to every creak. 'Goodnight, James,' she said with a wistful smile, and turned and went into her room, closing the door softly.

She heard his close, then his quiet tread as he walked to the connecting door.

It opened to reveal him standing there. 'Don't I get a kiss goodnight?' he whispered gruffly.

She couldn't resist him. She didn't *want* to resist him. She went into his arms, slid hers up round his neck and threaded her fingers through that irresistible hair. His mouth found hers, tasting faintly of cocoa and cream, and she sighed and leant against him.

She never meant the kiss to escalate out of control, but as their bodies touched through the thin barrier of their clothes the heat exploded between them. With a deep, muffled groan James anchored her head with one hand, hauled her up against him with the other and plundered her mouth until she thought her legs would melt.

She squirmed closer, a little whimper of frustration escaping from her throat, and she felt a great shudder go through James. His arms loosened, his mouth softened and lifted, his kisses becoming soft and tender, little butterfly kisses all over her cheeks and throat, and then finally he eased away from her.

She looked up into his molten gold-green eyes and was stunned by the longing she saw there. She'd thought her own need was great, but James needed her in a different way, a more fundamental way, as if his very soul would wither without her.

I love you...

Had she said the words? Had he? Or had they merely hovered on the tip of her tongue?

'Goodnight, Mary Poppins. I'll dream of you,' he murmured, and then, stepping back, he closed the door with a quiet but definitive click.

He must be crazy. He had been safely at work, out of reach of this siren with her soft voice and womanly body and generous mouth. A groan dragged itself up from his boots and he rolled his face into the pillow and muffled it in the nick of time.

He wanted her. She was just a pace or two away, just on the other side of the door—the door that taunted him. It would stay shut. He knew that, and so did Poppy. He wondered if she also realised that once they were home the story might be quite different. There were no doors there that would keep them apart. Once they were asleep the boys were out for the count. Would he be able to resist Poppy then?

Did he want to? Did *she* want him to?

He didn't know. He didn't think so, but then he remembered her mother, and the promise he had made her that he would look after Poppy and not have a short affair with her.

Was he ready to give her more? Did he want to? Did she want him to?

That was a quite different question, and one that filled him with doubt and concern.

Perhaps he'd better keep all doors shut, both now and in the future. He wasn't sure he was ready for the repercussions if any of them opened and he went through into an uncharted future...

The snow was wonderful. The strong wind had piled it up in huge drifts in the lane, and it was banked up in front of the tractor shed ten feet high, covering it to the eaves.

There was no way they were going anywhere, and Poppy was hugely relieved that it wouldn't be necessary to bribe Tom, because he was already giving her searching looks. In fact, she was surprised he hadn't said anything about the communicating door, but perhaps that would come later.

Meanwhile, she thought, the fates had played right into her hands with the weather. The wind had dropped, the sun was struggling to come out and if it hadn't been for the snow it would have been a lovely early spring day.

As it was, it was a magical world and one Poppy was determined they would enjoy. James and the boys would have a wonderful day together, and then they would have another evening with everyone gathered by the fire, with the family's gentle camaraderie to help him unwind and relax.

It was hard to get the boys to stay inside long enough to eat breakfast, though, and as soon as they had bolted their food they wrapped up well in borrowed scarves and hats and dashed over to the barn to see Hector. He had already been fed by Audrey at five, and would be due for another feed quite soon.

'Why don't we build a snowman first?' Poppy suggested, and took them up to the end of the garden where there was a flat lawn. There they rolled up huge balls of snow, piled one smaller one on top of a huge one, patted it down and smoothed the join, then found pebbles for the eyes and a stick for his nose and a slice of sugar-beet for his mouth. Poppy looked out an old hat and scarf and shoved a makeshift twig pipe into his mouth, and he was done.

'Wonderful. I wish I had the camera,' James said regretfully. Poppy went and found the family camera, and her mother took photos of all of them together, grouped round their snowman, and then more of the children having a snowball fight, and even one of James stuffing a handful of snow down Poppy's neck in retaliation.

One to show the grandchildren, Poppy thought wistfully, and wondered if there ever would be any or if she was dreaming.

Then it was time to feed Hector again, and then go inside for some hot chocolate and a slab of her mother's madeira cake, still warm from the oven and tangy with the juice of fresh lemons squeezed over the top as it came out of the oven.

After their elevenses they went for a yomp with the camera to see the spectacular ice-sculpture of the snowdrifts, and came back and listened to the news reports that declared Norfolk at a standstill.

'There. It's everyone—I doubt if you could have got to work from home,' she told James breezily.

He had found out that hardly anyone was in, Poppy

knew, because he had rung the office to check the situation. After hearing the news he seemed to relax even more, and threw himself into the day with renewed enthusiasm.

He stopped looking at his watch, stopped eyeing the phone and his car, and generally began to join in the holiday atmosphere with a vengeance. Poppy wondered how long it was since he'd had a holiday, and thought this probably counted as one of the few genuinely work-free days he'd had in years.

If so, then it was about time, and she was heartily glad she'd gone to the office and fetched him, however inadvertently. Quite apart from her own pleasure in his company, there was the pleasure of seeing him with the boys—and that, she thought wryly, was worth all the frustration and turmoil those altogether too brief kisses had wrought in her...

CHAPTER SEVEN

IT WAS early the following morning before Tom and
Peter got the tractor out and cleared the short stretch of
lane that led to the village. Once that lane was cleared,
James was able to get away fairly promptly.

It seemed odd without him, and yet in a way Poppy
wasn't that sorry to see him go, because she was finding
the nights a strain and the thought of another night with
him so near and yet so far had her climbing walls. The
boys, though, were in no hurry to get back to school,
and complained bitterly when Poppy insisted they should
return after elevenses.

'But it's not worth it!' George wailed, ever the vocal
one. 'It's only for the afternoon—not even all of it by
the time we get there! Can't we stay another night?'

'And get snowed in again, perhaps?' Poppy said with
a smile.

'Is it likely?' William asked, just a little wistfully.

'No. Come on, we'll feed Hector one last time and
then go. You'll be there for playtime after lunch if we
hurry.'

'We could play here,' George reasoned. 'And, anyway, Hector will miss us.'

'Bridie will miss us more,' William said unhappily,
fondling the dog's ears. She lolled against him, grinning
cheerfully, quite unaware of their impending departure.
Poppy felt a pang of guilt. Bridie was, technically speaking, her dog, although since she'd been away from home
her brothers had tried to train Bridie as a gun dog. How-

ever, she was useless, because she hated the noise of the guns, and Poppy missed her. Would James mind if she took the dog back to his house? After all, she'd suggested the boys could have a pet—

But Bridie?

Poppy swallowed. Would James be furious? He liked the dog, although getting him to admit it would be like pulling teeth. The dog, certainly, adored him.

Did she dare?

She went into the kitchen while the boys 'helped' Tom on the tractor, and suggested it to her mother.

'I think it would be wonderful for them,' Audrey Taylor said immediately.

'Even James?' Poppy asked wryly.

'Even James—perhaps especially James. I think it's a marvellous idea. Why don't you take her back with you today?'

'Won't you miss her?'

Audrey pulled the dog's long floppy ears lovingly. 'Of course—but then, so do you, and the boys are talking about getting a Lab puppy from the Bridgers. They've had gun dogs for years, and they don't seem to have untrainable progeny like this nitwit.'

Bridie lolled her tongue and looked cute, and Poppy laughed. 'All right, useless, you can come with me—but only if you'll promise to be good.'

Fat chance.

Poppy took the boys to school, then drove back to the farm and collected Bridie. The dog was delirious with excitement, a state in which she spent most of her life, and Poppy made her lie down on the back seat on a thick blanket and then, with the bed and bowls and blankets and lead and other endless bits and pieces loaded into the boot, they headed back to Norwich.

Would James be furious? Should she have contacted him? The trouble was, after a whole day out of the office and a late start that morning, she didn't dare interrupt him again. Oh, well, Bridie could always go home again if he *really* didn't want her...

James stood transfixed in the entrance hall. There was a frenzy of barking coming from the back of the house, and all across the elegant marble floor was a trail of muddy footprints. A blue blanket that had definitely seen better days was dragged half through the sitting room doorway, and the mortal remains of a cardboard box sat abandoned on the third stair.

'We don't have a dog,' he said under his breath, bewildered, and then, after a pause, 'Do we?'

His heart in his boots, he picked his way through the debris on the floor and opened the kitchen door.

Big mistake. A conker-coloured missile hurled itself across the room, plonked two great muddy paws in the middle of his clean shirt and washed him.

'Bad dog, get *down*!' Poppy yelled, and the dog dropped to its haunches, trailing mud down the front of James's shirt and trousers. Another suit that needed cleaning. He sagged back against the door and looked up, stunned, into Poppy's wary eyes.

'Bridie?' he said weakly.

'Mmm.'

Relief flooded him. 'Thank God for that. For a moment I thought you'd brought a dog home for us to keep.'

The boys fidgeted on their chairs and Poppy swallowed. James looked from one to the other and waited warily. Poppy cleared her throat and attempted a smile. 'Well, in a manner of speaking, I suppose I have.'

He felt the dread creep back again. 'You have?'

She smiled bravely, a better effort this time. She was obviously getting her second wind. 'Well—sort of. I thought we could try with her. We talked about the boys having a pet, and you seemed to get on so well with her. I didn't think you'd mind too much.'

His jaw dropped. 'A pet—?' He flapped a hand ineffectually, groping for control of the situation. 'I thought you meant a hamster or a goldfish—something small and contained, not—'

He looked down at Bridie, now sitting wiggling at his feet, tail swishing ingratiatingly, tongue lolling, eyes sparkling with untold mischief. He scrubbed a hand over his eyes and dropped it, and found a cold wet nose pressed into his palm. Without thinking he fondled her ears, and the tension seeped out of Poppy and the boys like air out of a punctured tyre.

He shrugged away from the door, stepped over Bridie's lashing tail and made his way to the table. A dog bed lay by the boiler in a little alcove that used to house—he couldn't remember what it used to house, but whatever it had been it was now gone, and Bridie's bed was installed there, for better or worse.

Oh, God.

He dropped into a chair, glanced at his watch and then again at the boys. 'Isn't it past your bedtime?'

'Poppy said we could stay up and wait if you weren't too late.'

He met Poppy's eyes, defiant and a little guilty. 'Using the boys as ammunition, Poppy?' he teased gently.

Soft colour touched her cheeks, and he knew he'd scored a direct hit. 'Actually, they were just on their way up to bed now,' she said quickly, with a look at the boys that dared them to defy her, and they vanished from sight.

'Mrs Cripps won't like it,' he said into the ensuing silence.

Poppy said nothing, and James got the distinct feeling that Poppy didn't actually care if Mrs Cripps liked the dog or not. In fact, since Poppy had been with them the place seemed cleaner and tidier than it had been for ages, so she was probably doing more than the rather short-tempered and stern Mrs Cripps anyway. She seemed to be coping all right with the twins. He wondered if even the amazing Poppy would be able to keep pace with the devastation of Bridie.

He looked down at the kitchen floor, covered in muddy paw-prints, and then at the perpetrator, who had slumped to the tiles by Poppy's feet, clearly exhausted by all that generation of chaos. Was she really here to stay? Poppy seemed happy to have her here, and the boys were certainly pleased. He sighed in surrender. How much havoc could one dog cause anyway?

'Poppy!'

Poppy's heart sank. She knew that tone of voice. After three days of Bridie in the house, she was used to James's yell of frustration when he discovered the dog's latest crime.

Yesterday she'd somehow got into the library, emptied the wastepaper basket and then eaten it. The day before she'd been curled up asleep in the middle of James's bed, the remains of one of his socks dangling from her lax jaws. Poppy wondered with a feeling of impending doom what today's little sin was.

She didn't have long to wait. James came bounding down the stairs, a pair of shoes dangling from one hand.

Oh, dear. He held one out to her and Poppy forced herself to look at it.

Oops. His dress shoes, now complete with—or rather without—mangled laces and with rather more ornamentation than before around the top of the toes. Her eyes shut and she forced them open again. Yup. Still the same.

She sighed, seeing her salary evaporating at a rate of knots. 'Sorry. I thought I'd shut the door.'

'Obviously not—unless she can open them?'

Poppy swallowed. 'Not knobs. She can push handles down, but she can't turn knobs.'

'Well, thank heavens for small mercies,' he said with a thread of sarcasm. 'Do you suppose we can manage to keep her confined, then? Or at least watch her? Is it too much to ask that I should be able to come home and find my home as I left it?'

Poppy sighed again. 'I'm sorry, I truly am. I will keep a closer eye on her. She's been allowed to get away with things. She needs a firm hand.'

James muttered something about not being the only one, and went back upstairs with his ruined shoes. Poppy went back into the kitchen, sank down onto the floor next to the dog, who was now sleeping, an expression of blissful innocence on her face, and stared balefully at the creature.

'You are a pain,' she said sternly.

The dog cracked an eye open and thumped her tail. Poppy resisted the urge to stroke her lovingly and tell her it was all right, because it wasn't all right. She stood up again, went over to the stove and stirred the pasta sauce. With her luck it would have burned and caught on the bottom of the pan.

James appeared at her shoulder and sniffed. 'Smells good. I'm sorry I'm not going to be here.'

She turned and looked at him blankly. 'You're not?'

He shook his head. 'No. Sorry. Another meeting with the Birmingham crowd, which starts tonight and will go on most of tomorrow, I expect. We've taken over the firm and slimmed them down, and we're just setting up the mechanics for expanding the computer notebook manufacturing part of the operation. There are so many changes and advances in laptop computers these days, and it's the place to be. Mobile office is what it's all about.'

'Pity yours isn't a bit more mobile—you'd be able to bring it home,' Poppy said quietly.

James sighed and ran a hand round the back of his neck. 'Look, OK, I should have given you some warning if I wasn't going to be here so you didn't cater for me—'

'It's not that,' Poppy cut him off quickly. 'It's the boys. It's Friday night, James. They've been talking about what you're going to be doing with them over the weekend, and I have no doubt it will be me that has to tell them you're not around—again.'

He let his breath out on another harsh sigh, and Poppy felt guilty for putting pressure on him. She should tell him it didn't matter, that she was sure he was doing his best to be with the boys, but the trouble was she wasn't. Oh, he thought he was, but couldn't they have scheduled the meetings for the week?

'Who set the meetings up?' she asked casually.

'What? Oh, Helen. She does all the scheduling.'

'How convenient,' Poppy muttered under her breath, and stirred the sauce so violently it splashed over the front of the pan and spattered her jumper. Tears of rage filled her eyes, and she snatched the teatowel from the rail and started to scrub at the marks.

James's gentle hands closed over hers and removed the teatowel, then used it to wipe up the sauce that had splashed her chin. 'Don't get mad with me, Poppy,' he pleaded softly. 'I am trying to be here as much as possible.'

'It just isn't possible often enough,' she muttered, headily conscious of the touch of his fingers steadying her jaw as he dabbed at her cheek.

'I'll wind up the meeting tomorrow as soon as I can, I promise,' he vowed, and the darned man managed to sound sincere.

Poppy scowled, and a fleeting smile crossed his lips. 'Don't frown, you'll get wrinkles,' he murmured, moving closer, and then he bent his head and touched his tongue to her top lip. 'Sauce,' he said by way of explanation, and then, without any explanation or excuse or justification, he lowered his head again—and kissed her.

Poppy forgot about the sauce, about the meeting, about being angry with him. She forgot about everything except the feel of his lips on hers, the touch of his tongue, the warmth of his mouth, the feel of his body under her hands. She would have forgotten her name, except James kept murmuring it against her lips, the soft whisper of his breath teasing her still further.

It was the ringing of the phone that brought them to their senses and had them moving apart like automatons. Poppy was sure her eyes must be glazed, and her lips felt full and puffy and curiously bereft.

She watched as James picked up the phone and muttered his name gruffly, then gave a short sigh and shoved a hand into his pocket. 'OK, Helen, I'll see if I can find it—oh, and by the way, while I've got you and the others aren't there, I'd like to get away tomorrow as early as possible—why? To be with the boys. Yes, I know, but the snow was hardly my fault and it was unavoidable. Yes, I know I didn't have to be there, but I was, and it happened—no, Helen, I wasn't exaggerating the situation,' he said with elaborate patience.

Poppy, eavesdropping shamelessly, thought she wouldn't have bothered to be patient. She would have told the bossy woman where she got off, and in no uncertain terms. In fact her hands itched to snatch the phone from James and do it anyway, but she resisted the impulse. She couldn't believe he couldn't see through the scheming witch. Very likely this meeting hadn't been necessary at all, or at least not at such length. Couldn't they have done much of the discussing over the phone with a conference call, or by fax?

Poppy ground her teeth, prayed for patience and stirred the spaghetti sauce—carefully. No way was she having James dabbing at her again, not until she had him to herself and Helen's phone had been disconnected so she couldn't interrupt!

He hung up but she kept her back to him, unsure how to react after that kiss. It had been superficially innocent, a fairly chaste kiss to the average onlooker. For Poppy, though, on the receiving end, it had been mind-blowing and leg-melting, and it was probably a good job he was going out tonight on second thoughts, because it meant she could sneak off to bed with a good book and take her mind firmly off Mr James Carmichael and his very kissable mouth...

'Poppy!'

'Oh, Lord, what now?' she muttered, throwing down the teatowel in her hand and heading for the stairs at a run. James's bedroom door was standing open, and so was the door to his *en suite* bathroom. The yells were coming from in there, so she went in, quite without thinking, and found James sitting up at one end of the bath, naked as the day was long, with Bridie bouncing in the water at the other end and chasing a back-scrubber round the bottom of the bath with her nose.

Poppy stood there transfixed, not knowing whether to feast her eyes on the sight of James's lean, firm body—and, yes, he did have hair on his chest, just across the breastbone between his copper-coloured nipples—or chase Bridie out of the bath.

Then the dog lunged towards James; he leapt to his feet and shot out of his end of the bath, and with a huge and very soggy leap Bridie followed him, stopped dead in the middle of the room and shook, just as George and William arrived, open-mouthed, on the scene. They dived for cover behind Poppy, and James made a lunge for Bridie with a towel in a vain attempt at damage limitation.

It was too much for Poppy. Clutching her sides, she sank against the wall, slithered down it to the floor and folded over in a heap, helpless with laughter. The expression on James's face was a gem, and she was sure he'd see the funny side eventually.

'Damned animals in the bath!' he was yelling, the towel now wrapped hastily around his waist. 'First the bloody penguin, now that wretched, festering God-forsaken mutt—!'

'She's not a mutt!' the boys chorused.

Poppy, sensing an eviction order pending, quelled her laughter, grabbed the wretched, festering et cetera, and ran for cover. Bridie thought it was a wonderful game, and bounced and twirled beside Poppy all the way down the stairs.

She stopped at the bottom to shake again, and Poppy was in two minds about sending her in to shake all over the pristine and tediously ivory drawing room. She thought better of it. The dog was on a sticky wicket as it was, without Poppy's help. She dragged her into the kitchen, rubbed her dry and tried to din some sense into her ears. The dog just grinned, tongue lolling, and then a moment later dashed to the door to greet James.

He was in a bathrobe now, firmly belted round his waist, his bare damp legs sticking out from under the knee-length hem. Poppy, stationed as she was on the floor, was in an excellent position to admire the firm, well-muscled length of his lower legs. However, she thought it might be a frightfully good idea to get to her feet, offer him a drink and an apology, and try and smooth the ruffled waters just a tad.

She stood up, screwed up her courage and met his eyes.

Was that humour she saw lurking in their hazel depths? She gave him the benefit of the doubt, and grinned. 'Sorry about that. I meant to warn you. We learned very early on to lock the bathroom door—Bridie loves to have a bath, and she doesn't tend to care if it's occupied already.'

It *was* humour. His lips twitched and he turned away, trying to maintain a dignified distance. 'I noticed,' he said drily. 'I don't suppose there's any point suggesting you take her to obedience classes?'

Well, at least he wasn't suggesting a one-way ticket to the vet, which under the circumstances Poppy thought showed remarkable restraint! She opened a bottle of red wine, poured him a glass and slid it across the table.

'Not a lot of point, no,' she agreed. 'We did try, once, but it was absolute chaos. We were asked to leave after two terms because she was distracting everyone. She just got so over-excited she was ridiculous. Mind you, she was only five months old.'

James eyed Poppy sceptically. 'But not at the end.'

She blushed. 'No, not at the end. At the end we just had to admit she's a waste of space.'

He gave the dog a look that was a mixture of exasperation and affection. 'She's very gentle and loving,' he said in mitigation, and Poppy could have fallen off her chair.

Bridie, as if realising that this was her big chance, sidled over to James, put her damp head on his knee and gave him her most appealing hangdog look. Poppy had to turn away, because he was so readily taken in by the scoundrel's transparent tactics.

Or was he?

'You old fraud,' he said lovingly, and scratched her soggy ears. 'Don't lean on me—oh, hell. Oh, well, it could have been worse. This towelling thing can always go in the washing machine. I don't suppose my suits are back from the cleaners, talking of Bridie's effect on my clothes?'

Poppy, biting the inside of her cheek, nodded. 'Yes. I picked them up this morning.'

'Perhaps I should buy a dry-cleaning chain next?' he said deceptively placidly.

Poppy, almost afraid to consider what Bridie would dream up next, thought it might be a good idea...

The weather was getting milder. Warm spring sunshine started to brighten the days, although the nights were still cold, and Poppy borrowed her mother's hatchback

so she could take Bridie out in the middle of the day
and go for long—and hopefully tiring—walks. She also
found the hatchback useful for her junk-shop and auction
finds for the drawing room, so much so that one day
James told her to take her 'company' car in to the
Mercedes dealers and exchange it for an estate variant.

'Obviously an estate car is going to be useful,' he said
with a shrug. 'You must have what you need to do the
job. Anyway, they hold their value well, so it's an in-
vestment. Just don't Braille park it too often.'

Poppy, who almost never felt her way into a parking
space, managed to hide her indignation. It wasn't hard.
She was too busy being astonished. She took the car,
changed it for a modest—by Mercedes standards—estate
car, and took pains to ensure that Bridie travelled on
rugs in the very back and didn't ruin it.

In the meantime she shopped for the drawing room,
kept Bridie and the boys on a short leash, and wished
she could find some time alone with James. He was
either in Birmingham, sorting out this new firm, or in
New York or Tokyo at a convention, or staying late at
the office for meetings. The promise in that kiss they
had shared at her parents' seemed destined to lie dor-
mant for ever.

It was perfect. Poppy stood back and looked at the piece,
and decided she couldn't better it. A lovely little
Davenport desk, with pretty drawers and gold-tooled
leather top, worn and ink-stained and carrying its age
gracefully, it was just what she needed for between the
windows in the drawing room.

The finishing touch to her revamp, she thought, and,
biting the bullet, she nodded at the auctioneer. Then
again, and again, and again. She swallowed. Had James

really meant her to pay this much for one piece? It was rare to find one so good, though, so genuine. She toughed it out, then, after it was knocked down to her, rang James from the foyer of the saleroom.

'I've just almost doubled your budget for the drawing room,' she told him.

'Is it money wisely spent?'

She laughed. 'I hope so—otherwise I'll be working for you for months for nothing to pay it off.'

'I hardly think that'll be necessary. If you're happy with it, Poppy, I'm happy with it. I told you that.'

Such trust. Was it unfounded? She hoped not. She had the little desk loaded into her car, wrapped it in blankets and told Bridie to lie down in the gap beside it, then drove it home. Would James like it?

Mrs Cripps was there and helped her unload it.

'Got brass handles,' she sniffed. 'Suppose I'll have to clean them?'

'Not very often,' Poppy assured her.

'Good, because with that idiot dog about there isn't time to do the basics, never mind any fancy polishing. If you ask me you're mad having a dog like that about the place, great useless thing that she is.'

Poppy hadn't asked her, but she had to say she agreed silently. Bridie was making an impact, all right, and it wasn't all positive. Why she'd bothered to bring the bed Poppy didn't know, because every night Bridie crept upstairs and slept on William's bed. They had formed an inseparable bond, and every morning, after she dropped the boys off at school, Bridie would station herself at the front door and wait. Only the promise of food or a walk would prise her from her vigil, and the second the boys were in she was glued to their sides.

She was at the door now, waiting, while Poppy polished the desk and slotted it into place between the windows.

It fitted perfectly, the wonderful patina of the wood set off to perfection by the pale walls and the warmth of the curtains. Poppy had relined them with a wonderfully rich floral fabric in a traditional country-house style, and they were held back so that the linings were revealed in a glorious splash of multicoloured splendour.

She just had the last window left to do, and after she'd settled the desk and admired it, she fetched the steps and put them up, then took down the last set of curtains. The linings were made and just needed to be slipped into place by hand, so she cleared the floor, banned Bridie to the other side of the doorway with a barricade and spread them out.

She had just finished the pinning when it was time to fetch the boys, and she brought them home, gave them a drink and a slice of fruit cake and sent them out into the garden with Bridie.

'Can we go in the woods?' George asked.

Poppy shook her head. 'Stay in the garden, please, so I know where you are, and keep an eye on Bridie. I don't want her running off.'

And she went back into the drawing room, settled herself down on a chair and began the job of hand-stitching the linings into the curtains. It wasn't a long job and she sewed quickly, and with any luck she'd have it finished by the time James came back from work.

Not that he'd be early. There was another meeting, she gathered. She glanced out of the window and saw the boys run past, Bridie bouncing at their heels. She smiled to herself and carried on with her sewing, and inevitably her mind drifted back to James.

Their closeness in February seemed to have faded

away. It was almost April, soon time for the boys to be on holiday, and their relationship hadn't moved forward at all.

Well, not as far as she knew. She still caught James looking at her sometimes, with a brooding, slightly thoughtful look, and she knew he was never far from her thoughts or feelings, but that didn't make a relationship.

She pricked her finger and swore softly, sucking it. Perhaps she'd stop now and go and check on the boys. She didn't want to bleed all over the ivory silk. Bridie would wreck the curtains quickly enough, she was sure, without any help.

She set the fabric aside and went through to the kitchen, snagging a jacket from the back of the door and shoving her feet into her wellies. She had her hand on the knob when the door flew open and William burst in, blood pouring down his face from a cut over his eye, and clutched at her.

'Poppy, come quickly, it's George—he's fallen out of a tree.'

And without letting go of her he set off at a run through the door, towing Poppy behind him. She tightened her hand on his and went with him through the gate at the end of the garden and into the woods.

Of course, she thought with a sigh, they would have gone in the woods. Why, oh, why couldn't they do as they were told?

William ran off the path and down a little track, and then slammed on his brakes and dropped to his knees beside his brother. Poppy, her heart pounding, dropped beside him and reached for George's throat to feel his pulse. Lord, he was still and quiet and white as a sheet apart from a glowing purple bruise on his temple.

Bridie was lying beside him licking his face, whimpering softly, and Poppy rubbed her head. 'It's all right, Bridie. Good girl. Stay,' she told the dog, and then, telling William, too, to stay with his brother, she ran for the house and grabbed the cordless phone, dialling 999 on her way back to the boys. She was almost out of range for the phone by the time she got back to them, but the ambulance station could hear her, just, and promised to send someone fast.

She sent William to wait at the gate, and a few minutes later she heard the siren and the swish of gravel, then the ambulance came into view, picking its way carefully over the lawn with William running ahead. Really, she thought, he should have been sitting down, quietly, having his own cut attended to, not chasing round the garden, but she didn't dare leave George. He was coming round slowly, still very groggy and weak, and Poppy was worried about him. She had never been so relieved to see anyone as she was to see the ambulance crew running over the grass towards them.

'Hi. What seems to have happened?' the ambulance-man asked.

'He fell out of the tree on me,' William told them. 'He was trying to catch a squirrel and the branch broke.'

'And you were underneath?'

William nodded.

'Right, let's get you two seen to, then.'

It didn't take long to load George into the ambulance once they'd fixed him on a board in case his neck or back was damaged, and after Poppy had shut Bridie in the kitchen and grabbed her bag, she jumped into the ambulance with the boys and they were on their way.

There'd be plenty of time to ring James once she got to the hospital. The most important thing was getting

George there fast. She put her arm round William and hugged him to her side, and silently promised them the biggest telling off in the world once they were both OK. For now, though, she just hugged and prayed and rehearsed what she would say to James.

Reality, of course, was unrehearsed and much more complicated. He was in a meeting, and the watchdog guarding him refused to disturb him. Poppy, remembering the last time she'd said the words, told the girl that the boys were in hospital and she needed to speak to him urgently.

A few moments later he came to the phone, his voice calm and unruffled. 'OK, Poppy, you've got thirty seconds. What is it this time? Another bargain antique? Or has Bridie eaten the stairs?'

Poppy swallowed. 'James, I'm sorry,' she whispered, her voice deserting her. 'They really are in hospital. George is with the doctors now, and William's waiting for stitches. I think George is OK, but he was unconscious for a while—'

'Unconscious!'

Poppy nodded, then remembered he couldn't see her. 'Yes,' she managed. 'But he's come round now—'

'Where are you, exactly?' His voice was sharp and incisive, and Poppy knew without a doubt that he would be there in seconds.

'Accident and Emergency department, the Norfolk and Norwich.'

'Stay with them. I'm on my way.'

He cut the connection, and Poppy cradled the receiver of the payphone and went back to William, who was sitting with a dressing on his head now waiting for stitches.

'I want to see George,' he told her tearfully.

'So do I. Let's ask if we can.'

She went over to the triage nurse and asked if they could go through and be with George. Seconds later they were ushered through to a cubicle where George lay surrounded by medical staff and nurses.

'Poppy?' he said weakly, and started to cry.

She took his hand and kissed him on the cheek, just below the black eye that was beginning to spread colourfully across his face.

'Are you his mother?' the doctor asked, and Poppy felt a shaft of pain.

'No,' she said calmly. 'I'm their nanny.'

I just want to be their mother...

CHAPTER EIGHT

FOR once in her life Bridie did nothing wrong. She was waiting by the door patiently when James and Poppy arrived back with a subdued and stitched William, and was overjoyed to see her young friend again.

While James packed a bag for himself and George, before returning to the hospital to spend the night at his son's side, Poppy settled William in bed and quickly threw together a meal for James.

He came into the kitchen a few minutes later and stared blankly at the plate. 'Poppy, I couldn't eat—'

'You have to.' She shoved him down in his seat and pushed the plate in front of him. He toyed with the food for a few seconds. He even got one mouthful almost to his lips before dropping it and pushing the plate away. He propped his head in his hands for a moment, then with a weary sigh he dragged his hands down his face and met her eyes. His own were tortured, and her heart went out to him.

'What if he develops a brain haemorrhage, Poppy?' he said apparently calmly, but his voice had a slight tremor and his hands were shaking. 'What if he—?' He stopped and sucked in a deep breath. 'What if he dies?'

She reached out and took his trembling hands in her own. 'He won't die,' she vowed fervently.

'Clare died.'

Poppy closed her eyes. She couldn't bear to see the pain etched into his features at those two quiet words.

'That was different,' she reminded him. 'She had a

serious medical condition which you didn't know about. It was unavoidable.'

'This wasn't, but it could still kill him.'

There was a hard edge to his voice that cut Poppy to the bone. She released his hands and stood up, going over to the window and staring sightlessly down the darkened garden towards the woods. 'I know. I'm sorry. Do you want me to leave?'

He was silent for a while. 'I don't know,' he said at last. 'I don't think so, but I don't know.' There was a crash as he brought his hand down on the table which made Poppy jump. 'Damn it, Poppy, what were they doing in the woods? Why weren't you there with them? That's what you're paid for!'

Her eyes slid shut, blocking out his pain because it hurt her even more than her own.

'I know,' she whispered. There was nothing else she could say, and another apology was so inadequate.

He picked up his plate and threw it into the sink, shattering it and spraying gravy all over the window. The fork bounced out and skidded across the kitchen floor, but Poppy left it, rooted to the spot by the anger and pain on James's face. He didn't look at her, just turned away. 'I have to get back to him. I'll talk to you later when I feel calmer.'

He picked up his bag and strode out, slamming the front door behind him with a resounding crash. She shut her eyes, the lids squeezing down and spilling the tears which had hovered on her lashes for hours now. 'Please don't let him die,' she whispered silently. Guilt swamped her, waves of pain and fear washing over her as she cleared up the mess in the sink and threw out the broken plate.

Then she went up to William, who was sleeping, and

sat beside him, fondling Bridie's ears and staring sightlessly across the room. George's things lay scattered all
about, his uniform thrown on the floor, his teddy half
hidden under the bed.

She picked it up and hugged it to her chest, wrapping
her arms round it and clinging to it like a lifeline. It was
only concussion, she reminded herself. It wasn't serious.
They were both being overdramatic, but because Clare
had died so suddenly of a brain haemorrhage it was hard
to criticise James for his concern.

She kissed William, tucked the quilt closer round his
skinny shoulders and went back downstairs, leaving
Bridie standing guard over him.

Why had she sent them out into the garden? She might
have known they'd disobey her and go in the woods.
Common sense dictated that she couldn't watch them
every second, but if anything happened to George common sense would be small comfort in her guilt.

The phone rang and she scooped it up. 'Hello?' she
said breathlessly, hoping that it would be James with
good news. It wasn't, it was Helen, imperious as always.

'Oh, Poppy, put James on, would you?' she ordered
casually.

Poppy counted to five. 'I'm sorry, he's at the hospital.'

'Damn. Has he got his mobile? I'll ring him there,
otherwise I'll have to phone the ward. Which ward is
the child on?'

'I'm not sure,' Poppy lied, 'but in any case I don't
think you can contact him tonight.'

'Why ever not?' she asked, astonishment evident in
her voice.

'Because this is more important,' Poppy gritted
crossly.

Helen laughed. 'Not than me, dear. I'll ring him there—'

'Don't. He hasn't got time for whatever you want to talk to him about.'

The silence was cold and stretched endlessly. 'Are you trying to prevent me from contacting him?' Helen said at last.

'Yes. Is it more important than the life of his son?'

Helen's brittle laugh made Poppy want to scream. 'Well, of course not, but there are shades in between, you know, Poppy dear. You young things are always so dramatic—'

'You're talking like a grandmother,' Poppy said calmly. 'Whatever it is you need him for, why can't you just do it yourself?'

'Because I need to talk to him—to sound him out. I know you're trying to protect him but there are things to decide, things you couldn't possibly understand,' she told Poppy, sounding like a patronising social worker talking to a delinquent.

'So decide, but do it on your own,' Poppy said ruthlessly, irritated by the woman's tone. 'I'm sure you're qualified to do so—why else would James have employed you and given you a position of such authority?'

'But I need—'

'Tough,' Poppy snapped, her patience at an end. 'Either make the decision alone, or wait for James. Just now he needs to be left alone.'

'Ignorant girl,' Helen muttered, just as the connection was severed with a crash. Poppy rubbed her ear and glared at the phone. Ignorant, indeed! Helen was the ignorant one—ignorant of the children's needs, of James's needs, manipulating and engineering time with him at the expense of his family life—

Poppy stormed through into the kitchen, ripped open the cupboard doors and emptied the contents out all over the floor. Banishing Bridie to her bed, she attacked the cupboards, restacked them and then started on the wall units.

Two hours later the kitchen was gleaming inside and out, and Poppy was still seething a little. Had Helen tried to contact James at the hospital? Probably.

'Damn her!' Poppy growled, and stomped across to the drawing room. While William was safely asleep she'd finish the curtains and rehang them, and the room would be as good as finished—not that James would appreciate it, considering what had happened to George while she'd been busy in there.

She had the cordless phone with her and kept looking at it, willing it to ring. Should she call the hospital and ask how George was? She didn't like to disturb them by making the phone ring on the quiet ward in the middle of the night, but the suspense was killing her.

She'd just put the curtains aside and was reaching for the phone when it rang anyway. She grabbed it, her heart in her mouth.

'Poppy? It's James.'

She swallowed. 'How is he?' she forced herself to ask, afraid to hear the answer.

'OK. Better. They've done a scan and there's no sign of haemorrhage or anything untoward. No swelling, nothing to concern them at all, and apart from feeling a little bit sick he seems fine. He's asleep now.'

Poppy couldn't speak. Her throat was clogged with tears, her whole body was shaking and she thought she was about to collapse.

'Poppy? Are you still there?'

She sat down on the sofa with a plonk. 'Yes—yes, I'm still here.'

'They're going to review him in the morning but they'll probably let him home before lunch.'

'Good. Do you want me to come and relieve you in the morning so you can get to work?'

'Work?' he said incredulously, as if she'd suggested he might want to go and catch some foul disease. 'Poppy, there's no way I'm leaving his side until he's back to normal. I'll bring him home and stay with him and William until they've both recovered.'

Poppy couldn't have been more surprised if he'd told her he was going to live on the moon. What had happened to the father who had never had time for his sons? Had she really managed to get through to him, or was it the threat to one of his sons that had finally reached him and made him realise how precious they were?

Whatever the reason, he seemed to have finally got there, and Poppy could only be grateful for the boys' sake. 'I'll see you in the morning, then,' she said quietly.

'Yes. How's William?'

'Fine. Sleeping.'

'Good. Any calls?'

'Helen. She was going to ring you. I tried to talk her out of it.'

There was a second or two of silence, as if she'd said something unexpected, and then he repeated that he'd see her in the morning and put the phone down.

She sat looking at the receiver blankly for a moment. Had James disapproved of her trying to put Helen off? She sighed heavily. 'I don't know, I can't do right for doing wrong,' she muttered under her breath, and went back to her curtains.

It was nearly three o'clock in the morning before she

finished them and hung them up, but it was worth it. They looked wonderful, and the room was now complete except for the carpet, which was being cleaned and repaired at a specialist cleaners before being delivered.

Tired but still not sleepy, she made herself a drink and went up and checked William again before going into her flat and leaving the doors open, as she did when James was away.

At four-thirty, when she was still restlessly fidgeting, William crept into bed beside her and snuggled into her arms. 'My head hurts,' he whispered.

'Does it, darling? I'm sorry.' She kissed his brow gently, just beside the stitches, and snuggled him even closer. 'Want me to tell you a story?'

'Mmm.'

So Poppy, ever the storyteller, invented a story about a little boy called William who went on an adventure and found he'd got a twin.

'And they all lived happily ever after,' she finished.

'Is that all?' he mumbled.

'Mmm. Go back to sleep, I've got you.'

'How's George?' he asked round a yawn.

'George is fine. Your father rang to say they'll probably be home in the morning.'

'Good. I miss him,' William mumbled sleepily, and, snuggling into Poppy's arms, he fell asleep.

Bridie crept onto the bed, curled into a ball against Poppy's feet and immediately started to snore, and within seconds Poppy, too, had fallen heavily asleep.

That was how James found them at seven-thirty when he came home to shower and change. He had gone into William's bedroom and found him missing, and blind panic had sent him racing for Poppy's room, only to find his son there curled up asleep in Poppy's arms, the dog sprawled across the foot of the bed, tail wagging a welcome.

Relief sapped his strength and he sagged against the doorframe and scrubbed a hand over his eyes. He hadn't slept all night, and his worry about George had been peppered with anger at Poppy and anger at the boys. She should have been with them, but equally they should have obeyed her, and if they hadn't that was probably his fault for bringing them up wrong.

Hence he was also angry with himself, and the boiling cauldron of emotion was killing him.

It was killing Poppy, too, he could see that. Her cheeks were streaked with tearstains, and he felt a pang of guilt for the way he'd spoken to her last night.

Ah, well. Nobody was perfect. He gave William one last lingering look to reassure himself that he was all right, then, shouldering himself away from the doorframe, he went through into his bedroom, tugged off his clothes and went into the bathroom.

The shower was hot, pelting him with scalding rain that washed away the fears and emotions of the night and left him feeling clean inside and out. He shut off the spray, snagged a towel from the towel rail and rubbed himself briskly dry, then went through into the bedroom to find some fresh clothes.

He had taken one step before he came to a grinding halt.

Poppy, sleep-rumpled and delectable, was perched on the edge of his big, high bed, her red-rimmed eyes widening at the sight of him. Soft colour flooded her cheeks as she turned away, and he hooked the dressing gown off the back of his bedroom door and shrugged into it, then went over and sat beside her.

'How is he?' she asked quietly, her voice subdued.

'Fine. Sleeping peacefully. I'm going back in a minute. How's William?'

'He couldn't sleep.'

'Nor could I.'

Poppy gave him a shaky smile. 'Me neither.' Her fingers twisted into a knot in her lap. 'James, I'm so sorry—'

He laid a hand over the tangle of fingers and squeezed gently. 'It's just one of those things, Poppy. George told me you'd ordered them to stay away from the woods. He said it was all his own fault—'

'He's eight,' she said, her voice anguished. 'How can he be expected to obey when faced with such temptation? They love the woods. They go in there whenever I'll let them. I should have realised it wasn't fair to trust them—'

'Poppy, stop it. There's no real harm done—'

'How can you say that?' she whispered wildly, turning her face up to his. Her eyes were huge, drenched with tears she was struggling not to shed, and James gave in to the urge and pulled her into his arms.

'Hush, sweetheart,' he murmured, and then the stiffness went out of her spine and she sagged against him, shaken with sobs she'd held in for hours.

After a few seconds she pulled away, though, scrubbing her cheeks with her hands, and he passed her a tissue. She stood up, walking away from him, and mopped herself up. 'I'm sorry,' she mumbled. Then she turned to him, her eyes like rain-drenched cornflowers in her pale face.

'So do you want me to leave?' she asked quietly.

'No. Perhaps I'm just talking myself into it because I want you here, but I honestly believe it was a genuine accident and that you didn't do anything wrong. It was just as likely to have happened with me looking after them.'

'But it was me, not you. That must be different.'

'Maybe. Whatever, it was a genuine mistake. I'm sure it won't happen again and anyway the boys need you.' I need you, he nearly added, but stopped himself in time. He didn't want to confuse the issue, and his emotions were strung out enough without adding to his problems.

'However,' he went on after a moment, 'I think it might be a good idea if you went home for a couple of days. I have to go to Birmingham again this weekend and I'll need you to cover for me then, so if you wouldn't mind having the time off in lieu, as I'll be here to look after the boys...'

She turned towards him, arms wrapped defensively round her waist, and nodded. 'Of course. I'll go when you get back with George.'

She looked so lost and small he wanted to drag her into his arms. Bad move. His libido, ever active despite the lack of sleep, was kicking into gear at the sight of her in that skimpy nightshirt, her hair tousled and her bottom lip soft and full and somehow vulnerable. He had to get her out of here, and fast, he thought, before he lost it totally and did something stupid, like drag her into the middle of his bed and make love to her till she wept for mercy.

'You can go now,' he said, a little curtly. 'I'll take William in with me—George misses him. If you could wake him up, you can go as soon as you like.'

Confusion flickered in her eyes, and then with a brisk nod she turned and all but ran out of the room, leaving him restless and dissatisfied and pricked by his conscience...

*   *   *

She didn't understand. One minute he was holding her and soothing her, the next he was sending her home as if he couldn't stand the sight of her. She woke William gently, sent him into his room to get ready and threw some clothes into a case. She had to get out now, before her control slipped again and she howled her eyes out all over him.

'Off now?' he said from the doorway.

'Mmm. When do you want—when should I come back?' she amended quickly.

'Friday morning? I'll take the rest of the week off, but I'll need to pop into the office on Friday before we go away.'

'Fine.' She looked anywhere but at him, grabbing her case and heading for the door. He stopped her just as she was about to squeeze past him.

'Don't blame yourself,' he said softly.

But she did, and she couldn't stay and argue the toss with him any longer because her eyes were about to leak and she was losing her grip fast.

'Give George my love,' she mumbled, and shot past him, down the stairs and out of the back door before he could stop her again, Bridie at her heels. She went home, threw herself into her mother's arms and howled, then, over a cup of tea and homemade gingerbread, she poured out all that had happened.

'You do realise it's not your fault?' her mother said sagely. 'When I think of the things your brothers got up to—still get up to! You can't be everywhere at once, and if James asked you to do the drawing room then he can't complain that you were doing it.'

'I should have done it when I knew they were in-side—'

'And they should have done as they were told. Poppy,

it's a lesson learned, for all of you, and no harm's been done.'

Except to my relationship with James, Poppy thought, but said nothing to her mother, who saw far too much as it was. Instead she ate her gingerbread, licked her sticky fingers and curled them round the pretty mug, propping her forehead against the welcome warmth.

'Why aren't I a shop assistant?' she mumbled. 'Or a forensic pathologist, even better. They'd all be dead, already, then, and it wouldn't matter.'

Her mother laughed and hugged her, and she drained her tea and went out to visit Hector, now hugely grown and bouncing with health. Poppy wandered through the barn and remembered James kissing her there amongst the animals, and how cosy and right it had felt. He had kissed her upstairs that night, too, and, if they had been anywhere other than under her parents' roof, she knew the kiss wouldn't have ended where it had. Perhaps if it hadn't, if they'd been lovers by now, he wouldn't have sent her away.

She hugged her waist, trying to smother the pain his words had caused. Not the words even, really, but the tone, the way he'd looked away from her as if he couldn't even bear to have her in his sight. He'd tried to be fair and kind, but obviously his gut feeling was that he didn't want her around.

She was shocked by how much that hurt.

The next few days passed slowly, but then Friday morning came and she opened her eyes and felt the chill of judgement day creep over her. She arrived back at nine and let herself in through the back door, Bridie at her heels. They found James in the hall, emerging from the library to greet them. The light was behind him and Poppy couldn't see his eyes clearly.

'Hi,' she said. Her voice sounded strained and unnaturally dead. 'Where are the boys?'

'I took them to school—the GP said they were fine,' he told her.

Poppy's doubts surged to the surface. Perhaps he'd sent them back to school so they wouldn't be here when he told her to leave. Maybe he wanted her to pack her case and be gone before they got home—

'Poppy?'

She looked up at him, still unable to read his eyes. 'Yes?'

'You did the drawing room.'

Here we go, she thought, and readied herself for the blow. 'Yes, I did—'

'It's beautiful.'

Her jaw sagged a little. 'Aren't you angry? I was doing it when George fell—I thought you'd be so furious about that that you'd hate it.'

He smiled slightly. 'No. No, I'm not furious. Not any more. I talked to the boys at some length, and they were adamant it was their own fault and they disobeyed you. I just want to forget all about it, Poppy.'

She stared at him in astonishment. 'You don't want me to leave?'

He looked down at his hands, studying them thoughtfully for a moment. 'Of course not,' he murmured. 'Poppy, I never wanted you to leave.'

'But I thought—you seemed so angry.'

'Poppy, forget it. It's all over—and I love what you've done in the drawing room. The only problem is the carpet. It came yesterday, and I've put it down, but I'm not sure if it's in the right place.'

He dropped his arm casually around her shoulders and led her into the drawing room, then released her and asked her what she thought.

She couldn't think. She was speechless, still trapped by the feel of his arm around her, even though it was gone. She forced herself to concentrate on the antique carpet he had set between the chairs and sofas in the centre of the room, exactly as she would have done.

'It's perfect. It looks lovely. Are you pleased with it?'

'I'm pleased with all of it. It's wonderful—warm and colourful and welcoming. Thank you, Poppy.'

And with that he drew her gently into his arms and kissed her lightly on the lips.

Her breath jammed in her throat, and as he lifted his head she looked up into the mellow green-gold of his eyes. Something flickered in them briefly, and then his lids grew heavy and his mouth met hers again hungrily.

'Poppy,' he said raggedly, and then, gathering her closer into his arms, he pulled her hard up against him so she could feel every rib against hers, every shift of his chest, every beat of his heart. One hand slid down her back and eased her hips closer, and a shock wave of desire crashed through her.

Now, she thought. Please, James, no—

He lifted his head and propped it against hers, his breath brushing against her face in broken shudders. 'I have to go,' he muttered, and eased away from her.

A soft moan of regret escaped from her chest, and he swallowed hard. 'Poppy, don't. I have to be in Birmingham by lunchtime, and it's ten now and I've still got to go to the office.' He closed his eyes and hugged her briefly, then let her go and turned away. 'I'll see you on Sunday evening,' he said in a strangled voice, and then strode across the hall, picked up a case from by the door and let himself out without a backward glance.

He rang on Saturday evening about seven-thirty, and her pulse rocketed.

'Hi,' she said softly.

'Hi. How are the boys?'

'Fine,' she assured him. 'George is still quite tired, but William is definitely up and running. I'm afraid they're in bed now, if you were ringing to speak to them.'

'No, actually, I wanted to talk to you,' he told her, and her stupid heart started racing again. Was he calling to chat to her? It seemed not, despite the eager response of her heart. No, what he was calling for was to ask if she had any plans for the following weekend.

'Not particularly. Why?' she asked.

'I'd like to entertain this lot—put them up at a hotel nearby, but give them dinner on Saturday at home. Now the drawing room's done I feel I don't mind entertaining, but I didn't want to ask them if you didn't feel you could cope.'

'Cope?' She swallowed. 'What do you want me to do?'

'Act as my hostess. Cook, if you feel you can, or arrange caterers if you'd rather—just generally be there to give me moral support during the evening.'

'Moral support? You mean, be there with your guests—eat with you and things?'

He laughed softly. 'Of course—Poppy, I'm not asking you to be a domestic assistant. I'm asking you to be there at my side and help me entertain these executives.'

At his side? Her heart raced again. 'Sure,' she said when she could find her tongue. 'Um—how many?'

'About ten—plus a couple from the Norwich office and ourselves—oh, and Helen, of course.'

Of course. Poppy's pleasure dimmed, but she promised herself she wouldn't let Helen bother her. It wasn't Helen he had asked to act as his hostess, it was her, and she'd make darned sure he was proud of her.

And Helen—Helen could eat her heart out.

CHAPTER NINE

POPPY spent the week agonising over the arrangements for the dinner party. She decided that as there would be about fifteen or so people a sit-down dinner would be impractical, and so she planned a buffet, then presented James with the menu for confirmation.

'I've tried to include vegetarian and even vegan options, as you don't know the guests very well, and I've made sure nothing's got nuts in just in case of allergies,' she explained.

'Looks great,' he said with a smile, and she could have melted in the aftermath of that smile.

So, the menu was decided. Now for her clothes.

Hmm.

Well, Helen would be done up to the nines, of course, and, although Poppy tried desperately to convince herself that Helen's opinion didn't matter a tinker's cuss, there was no way she was going to let James down by looking less than her best.

She might be a nanny most of the time, but next Saturday night she was James's—what? Partner? Hostess?

Lover?

No. Not lover. At least, she didn't think so.

Hostess, though, and she intended to do it with style. In what, though?

She went home to her wardrobe and searched amongst the contents, and was in despair when her fingers closed around the silk crêpe de Chine. Her brow creasing, she pulled out the garment and stared at it in surprise.

Of course. How silly of her to forget. It was a daring creation she'd made for a special evening when she'd been with her previous employers, and in fact the children had been ill and she'd never attended the function with them. It was stunning, though, a very off-the-shoulder, slinky ankle-length little number, in deep sapphire-blue with a thigh-high slit and almost no back and precious little front.

Still, she looked amazing in it; she knew that. All she needed was the courage to wear it, but there was nothing else even remotely suitable, so it would have to do.

She packed it carefully, took it back to the house and pressed it meticulously, along with a dress shirt for James.

Then she shopped and cooked and cleaned, and pacified the dreaded Mrs Cripps, and on Saturday morning she dropped the boys and Bridie off with her mother for the weekend.

'Wish me luck,' she said to Audrey.

Poppy's mother smiled. 'You'll knock him for six,' she promised, and Poppy blushed and kissed her and ran.

There was still so much to do—arranging the flowers, making the desserts, chilling the wine, polishing the silver and glass, making the canapés—and by the time James arrived back at six-thirty she was exhausted, but the house looked immaculate.

He ran upstairs two at a time and knocked on the door of her flat. She was in there, lying on the sofa with her feet propped on the arm, wondering how she was going to stand up in court shoes for the next six or seven hours. He gave her a quizzical look.

'Everything all right?' he asked worriedly.

'Fine—except that my feet are killing me.'

He lifted them and sat on the other end of the sofa with them in his lap, and with strong, blunt fingers he kneaded the aches from her tired soles. She dropped her head back against the other arm and groaned.

'That's wonderful,' she told him. 'Don't ever stop.'

He chuckled, a soft, husky sound that rippled up her spine. 'Unfortunately I have to, or I won't be ready to greet my guests.'

'So cancel them,' she pleaded laughingly.

He gave her feet one last squeeze and stood up. 'Have a shower,' he told her. 'You'll feel much better.'

'Mmm.'

'Poppy? You aren't going to sleep, are you?'

She made herself sit up. 'And miss the party? I don't think so. What time are they coming?'

'Eight.'

She glanced at her watch, then forced herself to stand up. 'Right. Shower, change, put out the canapés and party. Come on—out, please. The caterpillar needs to turn into a butterfly and it takes intense concentration.'

He went, closing her door softly behind him, and she dragged off her clothes, crawled into the shower and turned on the hot spray. He was right, it did help. After ten minutes of being pelted with hot water she felt almost human again.

She washed her hair and dried it straight. There was no point in trying to do anything with it, the darned stuff had a mind of its own, anyway. She would have preferred to put it up, but since it wouldn't stay there it made more sense to leave it down and just brush it well. At least it didn't come out of a bottle, unlike almost every other blonde she'd seen recently—including the dreaded Frisbee.

She applied her make-up carefully, pulled on the tiniest little pair of knickers she owned, followed them with a pair of sheer spangled tights and then wriggled into the dress.

Oh.

Memory had failed her. The deep plunging V at the back was deeper and plungier than she'd remembered, and the single shoulder strap was an extension of a scrap of fabric that could hardly be dignified by the word 'bodice'. And as for the thigh-high slit—well, it was just as well that the tights were sheer all the way up!

For all that, she looked stunning. All she needed was the courage of her convictions. She put on her shoes, straightened her shoulders and looked again in the mirror.

The dress was a wonderful fit, at least. Quite apart from which, it was the only thing she owned that was even remotely suitable.

She bolted down the stairs before her courage failed, and was in the kitchen putting out the canapés when James came in.

'Poppy, could you help me with my cufflinks? I can never get the damn things—'

He faltered in the doorway, transfixed, his eyes raking over her from head to toe.

'Poppy?' he croaked.

She took one look at his stunned face and shook her head. 'I'll change—'

'Will you, hell. Turn round.'

She turned, revolving slowly, his eyes burning a trail over her skin. When she was all the way round she forced herself to meet his eyes, and the look in them sent hot colour flooding to her cheeks.

'I'll change,' she repeated.

'No. You look—' He swallowed. 'You look incredible, Poppy. Absolutely stunning. Don't you dare change.'

'You don't think it's too much?' she said doubtfully.

He almost choked. 'Too much? If that's too much I'd hate to see you in too little.' He laughed softly. 'In fact, that's a lie. I'd love to see you in too little, but thinking about it now won't do my blood pressure any good at all.' He ran a critical eye over her again and nodded his approval. 'You look good—very good. It's an excellent fit. Whoever made it is a real craftsman.'

She blushed again. 'Thank you. I did try.'

His brows creased. 'You made it?'

'A year ago, in London. I've never worn it before, though.'

'Good. Then nobody else has danced with you in it.'

She shook her head.

'In that case,' he said slowly, 'I hope you'll do me the honour of allowing me to dance with you in it later— much, much later.'

The promise in his eyes was nearly her undoing. If the guests hadn't been due to arrive at any minute, Poppy doubted if she could have resisted the invitation in those green-gold depths.

As it was, she turned away and fiddled with the trays of nibbles again.

'I'll do my own cufflinks—I don't trust myself that near you,' James said a little gruffly, and left the room.

Poppy sagged against the wall, closed her eyes and counted to ten. Whatever had happened in their relationship before now, she knew that this evening signalled a turning point, and that tonight they would move on to the next stage.

A shiver of anticipation ran over her skin, and, putting

the thought aside, she took the trays of canapés through to the drawing room, set them down on tables and dragged in a calming breath, just as the doorbell rang for the first guests.

Helen, of course, waited a little while before appearing, in order to make an entrance. Poppy wondered if her nose was put out of joint by not being asked to hostess the function, but she probably imagined Poppy was just going to skip around in a black miniskirt and frilly apron.

Wrong.

In fact, Helen's entrance was spoiled by two things. One was her first sight of Poppy, that made her eyes all but stand out on stalks.

The second was her first sight of the drawing room, and that nearly took her breath away.

'James!' she wailed. 'What ever have you done?'

He smiled. 'Lovely, isn't it? Poppy did it for me.'

'But all this vulgar colour—!'

'Mmm. It looks almost alive now. Before it reminded me of nothing so much as the lining of an elaborate coffin.'

Poppy moved quickly out of earshot before she disgraced herself by crowing with delight. If Helen hated it, then it must have worked! She went back to her other guests, mingling naturally with them, talking and laughing and replenishing plates and glasses, getting to know the movers and shakers of the firm James had recently acquired.

They were nice people, decent men and women, their wives and husbands put at ease by the relaxed atmosphere Poppy tried to create. The soft music, the warmth of the surroundings—even if Helen hated it—all served to relax their guests.

Poppy herself, although she didn't realise it, was one of the reasons the guests were enjoying themselves so much. She was warm and natural, friendly, and above all genuinely interested in everyone, and it showed. They responded to her warmth like flowers in the sunshine, opening up and flourishing, and it didn't go unnoticed.

James caught her eye over and over again, smiling encouragingly, one eye tipping in the tiniest wink, and through it all a latent promise flickered in those green-gold depths. Later, he seemed to say.

Later...

'Lovely dress, but it's very daring for you, Poppy, dear.'

Poppy's exposed skin chilled at the icy tone of Helen's voice. Her chin rose a fraction, and over Helen's shoulder she saw James wink at her again. It gave her courage.

'Not really,' she replied. 'I believe in dressing for the occasion. This occasion called for something a little special, I thought.' She ran an eye over Helen's undoubtedly very expensive and well-fitting dress. In its way it was no more daring than Poppy's, and she took comfort from the knowledge that her figure was better than the older woman's.

'You're looking very good yourself,' she added, trying to neutralise the situation.

Helen shrugged and laughed. 'Well, it ought to look good, it cost a fortune. I thought it was the most appropriate of my designer dresses—where did you pick that one up? I gather there's a very good second-hand designer dress shop in Norwich.'

That did it. Poppy abandoned all attempts at niceness.

'Really? I wouldn't know. This one was made for me

in one of those funny little London attics—you know the sort of place.'

Helen's eyes widened. 'You must give me the name of the designer, dear. I could do with something else.'

Poppy smiled. 'Of course,' she said airily, dredging up the first Italian name she could think of. 'Now, if you'll excuse me, I'm neglecting our guests.'

And ignoring James, who was choking quietly behind Helen, she smiled sweetly and walked away. Laughter was bubbling in her throat, and James followed her out to the kitchen and fixed her with a mock stern eye.

'That was naughty,' he told her, laughter still threading his voice.

'Mmm. Sorry, but she was patronising me.'

'Don't they make pizzas?'

Poppy smiled. 'Mmm. And ice-cream. Don't worry, I don't suppose she eats frozen junk food.'

He shook his head slightly, then trailed a finger along the diagonal edge of her neckline, teasing the skin with his light, seductive touch. Instantly Helen was forgotten.

'I want to be alone with you, Poppy,' he murmured softly. 'I want to slide that strap off your shoulder and watch this tormenting creation fall to the floor at your feet, then I want to—'

'Here you both are. James, Mr Bulmore is asking for you. Something about pensions.'

James froze at Helen's voice, then with an inaudible sigh he turned and smiled at her. 'Thank you, Helen. Weren't you able to answer his questions?'

'I think he wanted reassurance from the boss.'

She slid her arm through his and drew him away, and Poppy's hand came up and laid against her breastbone, over the place where James had touched her with such devastating gentleness.

With a ragged moan she closed her eyes and tried to quieten her breathing, but under her hand she could feel her heart drumming out its frantic rhythm, and she knew that nothing short of James's touch would calm her now. She dragged in a lungful of air, straightened her shoulders and went back to her guests.

They ate and drank and were merry until long after Cinderella's coachmen were scurrying about under the floorboards again, and then finally, when Poppy thought her smile would crack and her feet wouldn't hold her up for another minute, the party started to break up.

Compliments flew, and as they ushered the last of the guests towards the door Helen took James by the arm.

'Darling, I've been a bit silly and had rather too much to drink—I probably shouldn't drive tonight. Maybe I'd better stay—I've got a bag in my car. I had a feeling this might happen.' She simpered up at James—well, in fairness she probably didn't exactly simper, but Poppy didn't feel like giving the manipulative creature the benefit of the doubt.

Neither, apparently, did James. He smiled at the Birmingham firm's accountant, just on his way through the door.

'Mr Bulmore, I wonder if you'd be kind enough to drop Helen off at home? It's on your way—thank you, that's very kind. Helen, leave your keys with me. I'll have your car dropped off in the morning.'

He kissed her cheek, ducked the pouting lips and stepped back beside Poppy, her keys dangling from his fingers.

Ouch. If looks could kill, Poppy thought, but there was only one thing on James's mind tonight and there was no way he was letting Helen get in his way.

The door closed behind them, and James turned to her

with a slow, lazy smile. 'At last. And now, Poppy, my dear, I'm going to have that dance you promised me.'

He went back into the drawing room, put on an unashamedly romantic CD and drew her into his arms.

Funny. Her feet didn't hurt any more. Maybe it was because she was floating, drifting about two inches above the floor on a cushion of air.

His arms felt wonderful, bracketing her ribs, enveloping her in his warmth. One hand lay lightly splayed across her back, the other curved possessively over her bottom, drawing her up against him as he swayed to the seductive music. Her arms slid up around his neck, her fingers threading through his hair, toying with the soft, springy texture.

She could feel his heart thud against her ribs—or was it her heart? It was hard to tell where he ended and she began, and when his lips lowered and claimed hers, the line blurred even further. She gave herself up to his kiss, to the hot, velvet feel of his tongue as it searched the intimate secrets of her mouth in a kiss much deeper than any they had shared before.

Finally he lifted his head and looked down at her, his face open and hungry. 'I need you,' he said rawly.

Her fingers cupped his jaw, relishing the rough satin feel of the skin drawn taut over the harsh angles. 'I need you, too,' she told him with her usual honesty. 'Take me to bed, James.'

His breath hissed out on a sharp sigh, and for a moment he just stood there. Then suddenly she was in his arms and he was striding up the stairs with her cradled against his chest as if she weighed nothing. He shouldered open his bedroom door, pushed it shut with his foot and then came to a halt in the middle of the room before lowering her slowly to her feet.

Then he released her, standing back slightly and looking at her as if he didn't quite believe she was real. His eyes tracked over her in an almost physical caress, and Poppy thought her legs would give way. Touch me, she thought, and as if he'd read her mind one hand reached out and threaded through her hair, sifting it through his fingers to fall over the bare shoulder revealed by the outrageous gown.

'So beautiful,' he murmured. His hand pushed the strap off her other shoulder, sliding it down and giving a little tug when the fabric caught on the tips of her breasts. Finally it fell away, and his breath jerked in as if he'd been struck.

His hands came out and touched her, the caress like the soft lick of flame against her skin as he cupped her aching flesh. He was trembling, his fingers hardly resting on her skin, their touch almost reverent. Her eyes misted, and, moving like a puppet, Poppy fumbled for the zip in the side and slid it down. Released from its hold on her, the dress whispered down to lie in a shimmering puddle at her feet.

She stepped forward out of it, into James's waiting arms, and with a muffled cry he wrapped her against his chest and held her tight. He was fighting for control, she realised, his chest heaving, his legs shaking, his whole body humming with this ferocious passion that was threatening to consume him.

She eased away and undid his bow-tie, then the buttons down the front of his dress shirt. The last button defeated her, and with a little cry of frustration she tore it off.

That was it.

James's control, held by a thread, snapped like the thread on the button and he ripped away the rest of their clothes, scooped her up and dropped her in the middle of the bed.

'Hello, Tiger,' she murmured, a smile flickering round her lips.

'Poppy, don't tease me,' he groaned. He lowered himself down beside her and laid a trembling hand over one breast. 'So soft—so beautiful,' he whispered, his breath puffing over her skin like a warm summer breeze. Then he lowered his head, his lips closing over the aching peak, and suckled deeply. Arrows of white heat stabbed her.

'James,' she sobbed, and then his mouth was on hers and his hands were cradling her face, steadying her against the fury of his kiss. Their bodies tangled, limbs entwined, the rough texture of his thrilling against the satin smoothness of her skin. She arched against him, her hands shaking so badly she had to clamp them on his shoulders to steady them.

'Please,' she moaned against his lips, and he moved across her, holding himself back for just a moment more.

He lifted his head and stared down into her eyes. 'Look at me, Poppy,' he said gruffly, and then with one long, deep thrust he claimed her.

'James?'

He lifted his head and kissed away her tears. 'Are you all right?'

She gave a shaken little laugh. 'I think so. Are you?'

He rolled to his back and drew her into his arms again. 'I don't know. I don't know what happened there, but it wasn't what I was expecting.'

His hands smoothed her skin, the caress gentle, tender—loving. 'I knew you'd got under my skin,' he said eventually, 'but I didn't realise it was going to feel like that. I'm sorry, I'm just a bit—shell-shocked, I suppose. It's the first time in over five years that I've made love to anyone.'

Poppy propped herself up on one elbow and stared down at him in astonishment. 'What? You've been celibate for five years—since Clare—?'

'No. But it's the first time I've made love since I lost her.'

She searched his eyes and found tenderness and confusion. 'Oh, James,' she whispered, and, lying down so that he couldn't see her misting eyes, she pressed a kiss against his chest. His arms closed round her, his hands flat against her skin, cradling her protectively while the tears pooled in her eyes.

'You were wonderful tonight,' he said softly. 'The perfect hostess.'

She blinked away the tears. 'I'm sorry I was nasty to Helen.'

'You weren't nasty, and anyway she probably deserved it. She can be a little pompous.'

'Pompous', Poppy thought, was not the word she would have used. How about downright nasty? His hand trailed over her shoulder and she turned her head and kissed it, pushing Helen out of her mind. His fingers twisted round to cup her jaw, and, rolling her over, he brought his mouth down to hers.

Without warning heat flared between them, and with a ragged groan James slid one thigh between hers and rocked against her. His breath hissed between his teeth, and Poppy arched against him, welcoming him into her body.

This was where she belonged, here with this powerful and yet humble man who had so much love to give.

Please, God, let him give that love to me, she thought. Don't let him hide it away again.

He arched against her, crying out her name as the harsh shudders of his climax racked his body, and, as her own body contracted around him, her last thought as she felt the deep liquid pulse of his release was that they had taken no steps to prevent her from conceiving his child.

Please, God, she thought, give me his child to love, and then the passion claimed her...

CHAPTER TEN

THE streamlining of the Birmingham company seemed to take almost all of James's attention during the next few weeks. The boys were on holiday, and Poppy managed to hijack James for long enough to go back to the zoo with them and see the penguin they had 'adopted'.

He was fine, doing very well, and none the worse for his exploits, to everyone's relief. The boys wanted to stay for lunch, but Poppy was feeling a bit queasy and so they bought some sandwiches and ate them on the grass under a tree. It was positively spring-like now, the sun gloriously warm, and all the trees were in bud.

The may blossom was out everywhere, and here and there they saw late-flowering cherry trees with their wonderful pink canopies as they drove back to Norwich. The boys were chattering happily, quite different from the sinisterly quiet lads they had been on the day of the penguin's abduction, and when they arrived back they went straight into the kitchen and demanded food.

Poppy opened the freezer, took one look at the contents and ran out of the room, up the stairs to her flat and into the bathroom. James found her there a few minutes later, kneeling on the floor as white as a sheet.

'Are you all right?' he asked softly, crouching down beside her.

'Yes,' she mumbled. 'I think I must have picked something up.'

She let him help her back to bed, and later on when

he came up he brought her some soup and toast, which
she ate ravenously.

'Perhaps you were just hungry?' he suggested when
he came to remove her tray a few minutes later.

She nodded, too weary to think about it. He was probably right.

He perched on the edge of the bed and took her hand.
'Poppy, will you be all right if I go back to Birmingham
tomorrow? We've got some technical meetings scheduled in the factory and I ought to be there, if you can
cope.'

'I can cope,' she promised. 'I feel better now. I don't
know what it was. You go.'

So he went, and she did cope, but she found she felt
queasy for a few more days and the only thing that
seemed to help was eating.

That was easy. She ate, and she was fine. End of problem. She'd been getting a bit thin anyway, so she wel-
comed the extra pounds she put on. James, too, seemed
to welcome them, not that they had very many oppor-
tunities to be alone together while the boys were on holiday.

Then they were back at school for the summer term,
but still James seemed to be busy dividing his time between Norwich and Birmingham. On the rare occasions
they were able to snatch a few uninterrupted hours,
Poppy found that the loving they shared grew more
tender and magical with every touch.

She was sure James loved her, but he never said so
in as many words.

Come to that, nor did she, but still lingering in the
back of her mind was her conversation with Mrs Cripps
early on, when she'd said something about the previous
nanny. Had James had an affair with her? Quite possibly,

Poppy thought, but she didn't feel like coming out and asking James, and as sure as eggs she wasn't about to ask Mrs Cripps!

And so the nagging doubt lingered, and Poppy wondered if she was just the latest in a string of women who had taken the edge off James's loneliness.

If so, why didn't he take Helen up on her offer? She was certainly a very attractive woman, and Poppy knew for a fact that James would only have to crook his little finger and she'd come a-running. Perhaps she was too valuable an asset to risk disturbing the status quo with a dalliance?

Certainly she was taking James away from Poppy and the boys at every opportunity, and as spring melted into summer Poppy knew she had to do something soon. Quite apart from her own frustration and disappointment about the lack of time she had with James, there was another rather more significant reason why she needed her relationship with him resolved, and resolved fast.

She was pregnant, the baby conceived on that first wonderful night together. Her wish had been granted, and now she had to deal with the consequences.

However, knowing James as she did, she realised that if she told him he would ask her to marry him just to do the right thing by her and the baby. He was that sort of man, and if she allowed him to do that she would never know if he truly loved her or if he was with her simply because of their child, and she couldn't bear to live with him and love him only to find out perhaps years later that he had never really loved her after all.

No, she had to know one way or the other, and the only way to find out was to force the issue—but how?

In fact the opportunity presented itself quite naturally. The first weekend in June was the day of the church fête—called by her brothers the fête worse than death—and it was traditionally held at her parents' farm. Poppy always helped if she was around, and this year she had told James she needed the weekend off so she could run the cake stall and the tombola.

At the start of the week James announced that he had a series of meetings scheduled in Birmingham for the coming weekend.

'But that's the weekend of the fête!' Poppy protested.

'Fête?' James said blankly.

Poppy sighed. 'I told you ages ago I'd need the weekend off. I have to help.'

James looked helpless for a moment. 'Poppy, I—can't you take the boys with you?'

'Again?' she said drily. 'James, I've had one weekend off since April. Just one. I'm their nanny, not their mother,' she added gently. 'They need you—*I* need you—and you're never here for us now. We hardly ever spend any time with you because you're always in Birmingham.'

He rammed his hands through his hair and leant back against the sofa wearily, rolling his head towards her. 'I have to go, Poppy. The changes have to be overseen.'

'At the weekend? Every weekend?' Poppy sat forward. 'Tell me again, James, who does the scheduling?'

He shrugged. 'Helen, usually—Poppy, it's not what you think. It isn't like that. Helen and I—well, we aren't—'

He floundered to a halt.

'You aren't what, James? Lovers?'

He swallowed. 'Exactly. She just arranges the meetings for the only times we're all available. Perhaps because she doesn't have a family she doesn't see the problem.'

'And perhaps you can't see that she wants you, James.'

He shook his head. 'No, Poppy, you're wrong. You and Helen have never hit it off, I know, and I realise she can be difficult to work with, but you make it sound as if she's trying to take me away from you!'

The incredulity in his voice, more than his words, told Poppy that he really did have no idea of what Helen was up to. How could he be so dense? she wondered. Ultimatum time, she realised.

She drew a steadying breath. 'James, no matter what the reason, this situation has got to end. I love you, and I want to be with you, but I'm not going to stand back and be your nanny and mistress and take second place to your job or your business partner or anything else. Either the boys and I are the most important things in your life, in which case you have to start showing it by being here for us, or we're not, in which case I'm out of here because I won't be put on the shelf and taken down whenever your lust and your hectic programming coincide!'

He sighed harshly. 'Poppy, of course you're important to me—'

'Then start showing it! I'm going to my parents this weekend, James, to help them as I'd promised. Now, either you cancel your meetings in Birmingham or you find yourself another nanny, because something's got to give and I'm sick of it being me.'

And without another word she went up to her flat, closed the door firmly and went to bed.

By Friday she was convinced she'd lost. James packed to go to Birmingham, having told Poppy tersely that he was going and thought her attitude was unreasonable and that she had totally misunderstood Helen.

She had refused to discuss it any further. 'Go if you feel you have to, James, but I mean what I say. Let us down this weekend and I'm leaving you for good.'

'Poppy, please—'

'It's your choice, James,' she told him quietly. 'It's me or Helen. It's up to you.'

'But there is no Helen. I mean, she's not—' he shrugged '—we're not—Poppy, you're wrong.'

'Am I? I don't think so. You know where we'll be. The choice is yours, James. Either you're there for the fête or it's all over.'

His face hardened. 'You're being unreasonable.'

'No. I'm fighting for something that matters to me—and so is Helen. It's not my fault you're too blind to see it.'

And she called Bridie, opened the back door and went out for a walk. He was gone by the time she returned, and she went up to his room, threw herself down on his bed and howled her eyes out.

Please, God, don't let me lose him, she thought, and then wondered if she hadn't been too pushy. Maybe she should just have told him about the baby. It was a wonder he hadn't noticed, in fact, because she was starting to show quite seriously.

Her mother noticed, of course, the moment she arrived with the boys. She took one look at Poppy, sent the twins off with Tom to see the sheep in the top field and sat Poppy down in the kitchen with a cup of tea.

'When's it due?' she asked.

Poppy didn't pretend not to know what she was talking about. This was her mother, after all. Of all people she would understand. And so Poppy told her, 'Christmas.'

Her mother's eyes narrowed. 'Christmas? Looks more like October to me. Is it twins?'

Poppy lifted her shoulders helplessly, and then the tears started to fall. Audrey Taylor, faced with a daughter whose life might be in tatters, gathered her child and her grandchildren against her ample bosom and rocked them all gently.

Poppy wrapped her arms around her mother's waist and hung on for dear life. 'Oh, Mum, I've been such a fool. I knew it was going to happen, the signs were so clear—I should have gone to the doctor, or at least the chemist.'

'Unless you wanted this to happen.'

She stared at her. 'Are you crazy?'

'Does James know?'

Poppy shook her head. 'No. I wanted to know if he loved me for myself. I'm not interested in him doing the decent thing. I want him all or not at all. In fact, I've issued him with an ultimatum, and I think I've probably just lost him, so perhaps you'd better steel yourself to being an unmarried grandmother.'

Poppy's smile was watery and very fragile, but it was a start.

'Don't count your chickens. He may come through for you, Poppy, and even if he doesn't, it's not the end of the world. You know you won't be homeless, and your children will always be welcome here, no matter what.'

That set Poppy off again, and when she finally hiccuped to a halt her mother sent her to have a bath and change and tidy up her face before her father and brothers came back to the house and saw her.

She looked out of her bedroom window and saw Peter and her father setting up the stalls for the afternoon, and

the vicar was there unloading crockery, just as he un-
loaded it every year.

And yet this year, for Poppy, everything was different.

It might be the best day of her life, and it might be
the worst.

She pulled on a loose cotton dress that fitted where it
touched, in the vain hope that her little tummy might go
unnoticed, and went down to the kitchen to see what she
could do to help.

There were scones to bake and cups to wash, and the
morning flew by in a flurry of activity.

Then it was the afternoon, and the vicar was there
declaring the fête open, and Poppy's heart broke into a
million pieces because James was nowhere to be seen...

'Right, everybody, that's it for today, I think, unless
you've got anything else to add, James?'

He looked up at Helen, smiling at him tentatively, and
wondered how he could have been so dense.

'No. No, nothing to add. Thank you, everyone,' he
said, and turned to Helen. 'What now?'

The others filed out while she packed up her things
and fiddled nervously with a pen. Helen never fiddled
nervously.

'Well, I thought as we'd got nothing scheduled till
tomorrow we might go down to Stratford-upon-Avon
and go for a walk by the river—perhaps go to the theatre
tonight. It's *Romeo and Juliet*—''

'And do you have tickets?'

Faint colour touched her cheeks. 'They're holding two
for us, pending confirmation.'

'And then?' he asked gently. 'What did you have in
mind for us then, Helen?'

'I thought—perhaps dinner.'

'And then?'

Her eyes fluttered closed. 'Maybe—perhaps…'

He drew her into his arms and held her gently. 'No, Helen. I'm sorry—so, so sorry, but no.'

She straightened away from him, moving out of his arms, pride holding her rigid. 'There was a time when you didn't say no,' she reminded him.

'That was years ago, Helen, before I even met Clare. We were different people then, and it didn't work. Now we're poles apart. I've got the boys—'

'And Poppy.'

'And Poppy,' he said, hoping it was still true.

'Do you love her?'

James's eyes softened. 'Yes, but she's really nothing to do with this. Our relationship was over years ago, Helen, before I met Clare. My marriage changed me, and losing Clare changed me even more. Even if I'd never met Poppy, there'd still be no hope for us, Helen. I respect you, I admire you, and I'm very fond of you, but I don't love you and I don't want to spend my life with you. I'm sorry.'

'And you want to spend it with Poppy?'

'Yes,' he said softly, realising that it was true. All he had to do now was convince her—

'You'd better go to her, then.'

'What about tomorrow?'

She smiled wryly. 'That was just a ploy to keep you near me for the weekend. I can manage tomorrow.'

He gave her an answering smile. 'I'm sure you can. In fact I'm sure you can manage all sorts of things.' He took the tortured pen out of her hands and set it down, turning her to face him. 'How about managing the Birmingham end for me?'

'All of it?' Her eyes widened.

He nodded. 'I'm sure you're every bit as capable of doing it as I am—maybe even more so. I haven't got the mental energy to build up another company again. I've got other things I want to do with my life, other places I'd rather be.'

'Are you sure? I mean, about me taking on this place?' She gestured around her at the offices.

'If you are.'

Her eyes sparkled with the challenge. 'Oh, yes, if you mean it. I'd love it. I've drawn up some ideas—' She reached for her briefcase but James covered her hands with his, stilling them.

'Another time. I've got a deadline to meet and I'm cutting it fine as it is. Come back to the office on Monday and we'll sort out the details.'

She smiled, looking genuinely happy for the first time in ages. She didn't really want me at all, James realised with shock. She just wanted a challenge.

The revelation made him feel much better. He pulled her into his arms, dropped a light kiss on her brow and released her.

'Good luck,' she said with a little smile.

He grinned. 'Thanks. I'll need it.'

And he grabbed his briefcase and sprinted for the lift. It was too slow for him, and rather than wait he took the stairs instead, three at a time, then ran out to his car, jumped in and gunned it, dodging through the traffic. He made it to the motorway in record time, and then went at just a tad over the legal limit all the way back.

He passed the turn-off for Norwich, took the junction that led towards Poppy's parents' village and narrowly avoided running into the back of a line of parked cars in the lane outside the farm.

He tacked onto the back, locked the car and ran down towards the farm. There were signs directing people to the fête, and he went through the gateway, paid his fifty pence entry fee and pushed his way through the crowd.

There was no sign of her behind the cake stall, or the tombola, but he spotted her mother wielding a teapot in the big farm kitchen. There was a queue of people going in and out of the doorway, bearing cups and plates piled high with scones and cream and jam, and he joined the queue and fought his way to the front.

'Mrs Taylor? Audrey?'

She looked up and her face was wreathed in smiles. 'I knew you'd come,' she said, and passed him two cups of tea. 'Take that to Poppy—she's in the bric-a-brac. Mrs Thomas was ill.'

He didn't know who Mrs Thomas was, and without being callous he didn't care. All he could think about was finding Poppy before it was too late.

He took the tea, worked his way carefully out of the door and went out onto the crowded lawn. 'Where's the bric-a-brac?' he asked.

The elderly lady studied him. 'You looking for Poppy?'

He nodded.

'Up at the top end, by the rhododendrons.'

He thanked her and headed in that direction, dodging a group of Brownies dancing round a maypole, and finally he was there, face to face with her.

She looked at him, her eyes strained and wary, and he wanted to drag her into his arms and tell her it was all right.

Instead he passed her a cup of tea. 'Here—from your mother.'

'Thank you.' Lord, it was all so formal and polite, it

made him want to scream. She was wearing a pretty cotton jersey dress, and she looked cool and delectable. She also looked as if she'd been crying last night, and he could have kicked himself for hurting her.

'I talked to Helen,' he told her.

'Could I have this pot, dear? Thank you, Poppy. Nice to see you again.'

'And you, Mrs Wilkins.' She glanced back at James. 'And?'

'You were right.'

She gave a little huff of laughter and turned to take the money from the next customer. She dropped the coins into the pot and looked at him again. 'I know. So what now?'

'I gave her Birmingham.'

'Sounds a bit feudal. That will be fifty pence, please. Thank you.'

'Poppy, can we go somewhere and talk?'

'No, I have to do this—thank you. Hello, Mr Burrows. How are you now? Better? I'm so glad. Do give my love to your wife.'

The public address system spluttered into life then, and the vicar thanked the Brownies for their lovely maypole dance, and everybody clapped and cheered.

'And now I've been asked to tell you that there's five minutes before the start of the tug of war, so if you'd all like to make your way up to the top part of the garden and cheer on your villages, I'm sure they'd all be glad of your support. There are all sorts of games up there, as well, so plenty for everyone.'

The PA crackled once more and was silent, and James was just about to try and talk to Poppy again when it came back to life. 'Gentlemen, I've just been told that the home team are short of a man for the tug of war. Have we got an able-bodied volunteer in the crowd?'

Poppy looked at him. 'Go and do it.'

His jaw sagged. 'Are you mad? And, anyway, I'm trying to talk to you—'

'Later. Hello, Mrs Jones.'

James gave up. He put down his untouched cup of tea, shrugged off his coat and went up to the other end of the garden where he and the boys had made a snowman all those months ago. Tom and Peter were lined up with a few other strong young men on one side of the line, and they looked at him assessingly.

'Still need another man?' he asked.

Tom nodded. 'Poppy send you?'

He grinned ruefully. 'Yes.'

'Ever done it before?'

He shook his head.

Tom laughed. 'Poor you. Stick your jacket there and come and have a lesson.'

How hard could it be? He went over to the rope, listened to what Tom said, and then the rope was being picked up, James was slotted into the middle and the tension was taken up. He dug in his heels, threw his weight back on the rope as the whistle blew and heaved in time to the cox.

They won. It was a miracle, a masterpiece of sweat and guts and determination, but they won two out of three times, and were declared the champions.

There was much back-slapping and cheering from the crowd, and James looked up to see Poppy slipping away through the colourful throng.

Damn. He tried to follow her but she was gone, slipped away from him like quicksilver.

The PA crackled into life again, and he shook his

head, wondering if Helen would believe what he was about to do. There was no sign of the boys but he knew they were here, probably part of the cheering crowd. He went down the path towards the house, and in the door of the conservatory he saw the vicar.

'Excuse me, I want to contact Poppy. Mind if I use the public address?'

The vicar handed him the mike. 'Be my guest,' he said. 'Turn it on here.'

He took a deep breath, scanned the crowd and switched on the mike. His palms were sweating, his heart was going nineteen to the dozen and he thought he was going to die. He lifted the mike to his mouth.

'Poppy, it's James,' he said clearly, and everyone turned to look at him standing in the conservatory door-way. 'I don't know where you are. I can't find you, and when I can find you I can't talk to you because you're too busy, but I'm not a patient man, Poppy, and I can't wait.'

He cleared his throat and lifted the microphone to his mouth again. 'Poppy, I love you,' he said, and suddenly the crowd parted and he could see her, standing there on the other side of the plant stall, her hands over her mouth, her eyes like saucers. 'I love you very much,' he went on, 'and I'd be honoured if you'd consent to be my wife, and the mother of my children.'

Her hands dropped, fluttering down over her chest to settle against the front of her dress. Her face was alight with love, and even from here he could see the tears coursing down it.

'Is that a yes?' he said softly, and she nodded.

The crowd cheered, and, passing the mike back to the bemused vicar, he crossed the lawn at a run and swept up his bride-to-be in his arms, whirling her round before setting her down and kissing her soundly.

Poppy couldn't believe it. She was so sure she'd lost him, that she'd pushed him too hard and driven him away for ever, and now he was here, doing this! 'Fancy proposing to me over the PA!' she scolded laughingly as he let her go.

'It was the only way I could get you to listen,' he explained, and hugged her hard. 'Oh, Poppy, I love you so much. It was only when I thought about losing you that I realised just how much you'd come to mean to me—to us.'

She became aware of the boys pushing up beside them, their faces shining like beacons, and she put her arms round them and drew them into the embrace. Her parents were there, too, on the outside of the crowd, and her brothers, still carrying the jacket that James had abandoned before the tug of war.

'I think you two ought to go for a little walk,' her mother said, ushering everyone away from them. 'Go on, shoo. Boys, come with me and I'll find you some ice-cream.'

So they were alone, walking down the lane hand in hand, and Poppy thought her heart would burst with happiness. There was only one thing worrying her, and she felt she ought to get it out of the way. 'There's something you ought to know,' she told him.

'Sounds ominous.'

She gave him a wary smile. 'That depends on your viewpoint.' She took a deep breath. 'I'm—we're—having a baby.'

He stopped dead in his tracks. 'What?'

'In fact, maybe two. Mum thinks I'm a bit big for just one, as it's my first.'

He turned her to face him and looked down. 'Big? Two? When?' he croaked.

She smiled tentatively. 'Christmas.'

His face contracted a little, and slowly, cautiously, he put a hand out and laid it over the slight swell of her tummy. 'Oh, Poppy,' he said raggedly, and then he pulled her gently into his arms and hugged her. 'Oh, Poppy,' he said again, and then he said nothing for ages, just held her, rocking her, his hands curved protectively around her body, holding her close.

When he let her go his lashes were clumped together and his eyes sparkled with joy. 'When I lost Clare I thought I'd never love anyone again,' he said slowly. 'Then I met you, and it was like being brought out of the darkness into the light. I suppose that's why I didn't understand what Helen was doing.'

'Did you tell her?'

'About us? She knew. I think she understands now that I could never have loved her, regardless, and, to tell you the truth, I don't think she really loved me either. Maybe she thought she did, or maybe I was just another challenge. Anyway, as I was saying when you accused me of being feudal, I've put her in charge of Birmingham. We'll sort out the details on Monday, but it's right up her street. She'll love it, and it means I can take a bit of a back seat and spend some time with my family.'

'You mean that?' Poppy said doubtfully, hardly daring to believe it.

He tipped her chin up so she had to meet his eyes, and she saw all the love she could ever hope for shining there in their green-gold depths. 'I mean it. I've missed out on too much. I'm not going to miss out on anything more. I'm sorry, Poppy, for better or worse, you've got me in your life now for good.'

It sounded wonderful, but there was just one more thing. 'About your last nanny—'

'What about her?'

'Why did she leave?'

'She was pregnant—she and her boyfriend Todd had been a little careless—you know how it is.'

Poppy, her heart now overflowing with happiness, laughed softly. 'Yes. Yes, I know exactly how it is. So, Mr Carmichael, when are you going to make an honest woman of me?'

He grinned. 'The vicar's there—let's go and chat to him, see if he can sort out a date. In view of the budding population explosion, I think the sooner the better?'

Poppy laughed. 'If not before…'

EPILOGUE

'AND now, it gives me great pleasure to declare the annual church fête open!'

Poppy, trapped behind the cake counter, looked across the lawn and caught James's eye. He was standing beside her father, one chubby little baby girl on each arm, trying to hold a conversation against impossible odds. He excused himself and crossed over to her, leant over the counter and kissed her.

'Are they all right?'

'Yes. I'm practising being a new man.'

Her brows quirked together.

'Stereo nappy-changing,' he told her. 'I'm getting quite good at it.'

She chuckled and kissed her daughters. They gurgled happily and grabbed her hair, and she had to enlist someone's help to free her.

'That's quite a handful you've got yourself there, young Poppy,' one of the old faithfuls said.

'Yes, and the children can be quite difficult, too,' James said under his breath.

Poppy laughed and pushed him away. 'Go on, go and make yourself useful somewhere. I'll come and relieve you for the tug of war.'

He laughed. 'After this lot, it'll be a breeze,' he grinned.

Audrey appeared at her daughter's elbow. 'Everything all right?'

Poppy thought of her family: James, the boys—

George and William—the girls—Sarah and Hannah—
and Bridie, lying at her feet.

'Couldn't be better,' she said with a smile.

'The boys are growing up into nice lads.'

'Like their father—all any of them needed was loving.'

Audrey looked at her daughter and smiled in satisfaction. 'It hasn't done you any harm, either. You look
well.'

'I am well. Mind the stall for me, could you? I have
to go and watch the tug of war.'

They won again, which nearly caused a riot. James
escaped from the celebrations and came over to her,
grinning broadly.

'Hello, my hero,' she said with a chuckle.

'Hi.' He looked at his palms, and Poppy saw the skin
reddened from the rope.

'Ouch. Do they need some cream on?'

He shook his head. 'No, just a little bit of TLC. It
seems to cure pretty well everything.'

He lifted them to her lips and she kissed them gently.
'Better?' she murmured.

'Of course. You make everything better.' His eyes
softened. 'I love you, Mrs Carmichael. You're a miracle.'

She chuckled. 'Another one? Your life seems to be
full of miracles these days.' She glanced at the girls,
lying on a rug beside them, happily chewing their fists.

James's eyes followed hers, and his smile almost
melted her. 'It does, doesn't it? But they wouldn't be
here without you. You are without doubt the best thing
that could ever have happened to me.'

Poppy smiled mistily. 'Don't imagine a bit of flattery

and rope burn will get you out of nappy duty,' she warned him.

He chuckled. 'It was worth a try. I tell you what, I'll settle for more tender loving care from my own personal miracle…'

HARLEQUIN PRESENTS®

HARLEQUIN PRESENTS
men you won't be able to resist
falling in love with...

HARLEQUIN PRESENTS
women who have feelings
just like your own...

HARLEQUIN PRESENTS
powerful passion in
exotic international settings...

HARLEQUIN PRESENTS
intense, dramatic stories that will keep you
turning to the very last page...

HARLEQUIN PRESENTS
The world's bestselling romance series!

Harlequin® Historical

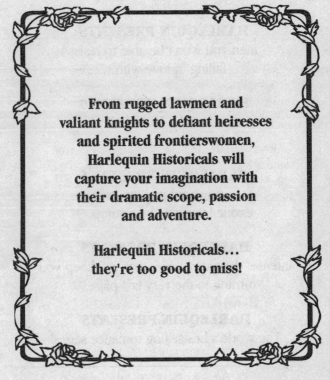

From rugged lawmen and
valiant knights to defiant heiresses
and spirited frontierswomen,
Harlequin Historicals will
capture your imagination with
their dramatic scope, passion
and adventure.

Harlequin Historicals…
they're too good to miss!

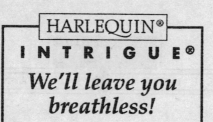

HARLEQUIN®

AMERICAN ◆ ROMANCE®

LOOK FOR OUR FOUR FABULOUS MEN!

Each month some of today's bestselling authors bring
four new fabulous men to Harlequin American Romance.
Whether they're rebel ranchers, millionaire power brokers
or sexy single dads, they're all gallant princes—and
they're all ready to sweep you into lighthearted fantasies
and contemporary fairy tales where anything is possible
and where all your dreams come true!

You don't even have to make a wish...
Harlequin American Romance will grant your every desire!

Look for Harlequin American Romance
wherever Harlequin books are sold!